# BURNED
with the
# COYOTE
# BRAND

Center Point
Large Print

**This Large Print Book carries the
Seal of Approval of N.A.V.H.**

# BURNED
## with the
# COYOTE
# BRAND

## A WESTERN TRIO

# Dan Cushman

CENTER POINT LARGE PRINT
THORNDIKE, MAINE

This Center Point Large Print edition
is published in the year 2015 in conjunction with
Golden West Literary Agency.

The text of this Large Print edition is unabridged.
In other aspects, this book may vary
from the original edition.
Printed in the United States of America
on permanent paper.
Set in 16-point Times New Roman type.

ISBN: 978-1-62899-596-1 (hardcover)
ISBN: 978-1-62899-601-2 (paperback)

Library of Congress Cataloging-in-Publication Data

Cushman, Dan.
[Short stories. Selections]
Burned with the coyote brand : a western trio / Dan Cushman. —
Center Point Large Print edition.
pages cm
Summary: "Greed, deceit, and betrayal are motivating factors in three
western stories where right needs to use a little might to come out on
top"—Provided by publisher.
ISBN 978-1-62899-596-1 (hardcover : alk. paper)
ISBN 978-1-62899-601-2 (pbk. : alk. paper)
1. Large type books. 2. Western stories.
    I. Cushman, Dan. She-wolf of the Río Grande. II. Title.
PS3553.U738A6 2015
813'.54—dc23

                                         2015007619

# BURNED
## with the
# COYOTE
# BRAND

# Contents

# SHE-WOLF OF THE RÍO GRANDE

# I

There were nine of them headed by a girl whose face was half concealed by a black leather mask. They had ridden from one of the steep, rock-sided arroyos that wound into the wilds of Chihuahua, and then dismounted, and hunkered on their boot heels, smoking countless hand-twisted cigarettes, waiting for darkness to settle over the Río Grande.

The girl stood apart, tall and slim-waisted, an arrogant leader of this catch-all crew—Mexicans with varying degrees of Indian blood, one a squat Apache renegade, one a lean, rusty-complexioned *gringo* named Alvin Tucker.

The girl waited, hand on the bridle of her rangy black stallion, until the degree of muggy darkness suited her, then she reached the stirrup and swung to the saddle, waiting for the others to follow her. She carried a long-lashed *cuerda* coiled in her hand, and signaled with that, swinging the stallion without a word and riding down through yellowish water and mud bars to the American side. There she sat, lithe and slim, looking at the rising country to the south.

Tucker, the *gringo*, spoke to the girl. "Never expected to invade Texas soil with a Mex army, but here I am. I hope you get us back, *señorita*."

He thought a second and added: "*Señorita* Hija de Satanás."

That name was like a blow across her face. She twisted the bridle and the big black stallion, responding to the unexpected strength that lay in her slim body, reared high and directly at the mustang Tucker was riding.

Tucker flung himself back and to one side, leaving the saddle. The mustang tried to get away and slipped doing it, almost pinning Tucker, then the animal lunged forward and away, running with head sidewise, dragging bridle reins. Tucker was on the ground, doubled up, unprotected, and for a moment it seemed that the great black stallion would trample him beneath his hoofs, but the girl ripped back, making him sink to haunches.

Tucker had lost his cigarette and his hat, but he still grinned while thrusting himself to a sitting position. "By damn, you can kill me for it, if you like, but they had a knack for names, those Chihuahua peons, when they tagged that name Hija de Satanás on you."

"You will not call me that again, *Señor* Americano!" Her eyes had fire through the slits of her mask; her lips were drawn tightly revealing the tips of white teeth. Her voice was tightly controlled and little more than a whisper.

"No, ma'am," said Tucker. He was a renegade and a killer like the rest, but he could admire high blood in a horse or a woman. "You're The Angel, now and forever."

The Apache renegade, riding long-legged, Indian-style with a cinched-on blanket in place of a saddle and an under jaw hackamore for a bridle, caught Tucker's mustang and led it back. Tucker got up with dirt and bits of grass clinging to him to take the reins. He was still twisting his thin, cruel face to one side, admiring the girl.

"The Angel," he said. "But I ask you, does a real angel act like that?"

She looked at him for a second, then her head jerked back and her thin, lovely lips twisted in a smile. She was contemptuous of him, contemptuous of them all.

A short, broad man whose ugly, clownish face had won him the name Paraso pointed off to the north. "Cañon Puerta . . . like so?"

She nodded, bringing to life the *jingle* of little silver ornaments that decorated the band of her black sombrero. She turned, and evening light struck her face revealing its loveliness despite the black leather mask that covered most of her nose and cheeks. She was tall. She wore a black silk shirt with more native-wrought silver spangles, with a *chaleco* of soft-rubbed deerskin over it. Around her slim waist was a heavy belt studded with silver and gold, cinched tightly to hold her forked skirt of Spanish leather. Actually it was more *chaparejos* than skirt, designed to turn the harsh thorn and burrs of the Río Grande country. Her feet were encased in tiny boots, intricately stitched and inlaid, and on her heels were big, dollar-rowelled silver spurs. She was armed, carrying around her waist one of the new Colt revolvers. It was long-barreled, and she wore it in a peculiar manner, high on the left side, its barrel slanting almost horizontally. From a scabbard beneath her right knee poked the stock of a Winchester rifle.

Paraso twisted his broad face in a grin and went on: "They will be waiting for us there, *Señorita* Angel? Those four hundred fat steers like *gringo* millionaire like for his table? In box cañon like you say with only three, four men for guard?" He gestured aloft with ring-decorated fingers. "What do we care for three, four men?" He pointed a finger. "*Ka-poof.* Bang! Three, four men."

Tucker said: "Don't finish them off too easy, Paraso, my boy. That Millerick plays his cards close enough. He aims on delivering those fat steers to a damn' Yank cattle buyer from Pecos, not a gang of wet-bellies like us from old Mex. Maybe there'll be a little of that *ka-poof* on his side, too."

"So much the better, *gringo*! Paraso, hees love to shoot. Especially *gringo*, Paraso . . ."

"Quiet!" The Angel spoke only the single word, and Paraso's voice stopped instantly although his lips kept moving, and he kept shaking his massive head, saying silent things about the *gringos*. The girl sat for a while, holding tight rein on her stallion, then she signaled with a flip of the *cuerda* in her hand, and rode away, her body, slim and supple, integrated with every movement of the horse.

She led them across rising ground to an arroyo whose bottom seemed to be impenetrable from thorn, but a trail opened at the final instant and she followed it, guiding the horse through night shadows, making every unpredictable turn as it took zigzag courses up the rocky side and down again until it finally reached a sort of rolling summit from which the whole country could be viewed in the light of the rising moon.

At their backs, shining like molten bullet metal, the Río Grande split and rejoined, making intricate channel patterns through mud bars, and beyond that lay the barren mountain and plateau country of Chihuahua. Ahead of them were plains and mesas, the no-man's-land of the Texas Presidio. From this view it seemed to be a lifeless country of sand and wind-blasted rock, but there were also valleys of lush green grass, and in one of them the Block M home ranch of Ross Millerick.

The girl pointed out some of the country's features, speaking in brief sentences, indicating the crooked trail that riders would have to follow in traveling from Cañon Puerta to the Block M for help. "Ten miles . . . by the straight line. But horsemen will have to go by Agua Nueva and back up Sarita Valley, so it will take four hours, perhaps more. They can't be back before dawn, and by then those Millerick longhorns will have the mud of the Río Grande dried on them."

It was not far to the Río, and beyond to the crazy-crooked cañons of the Río Jacinto, that devil's country of Chihuahua where five men could laugh at a regiment.

A little *bandido* spoke in a whining voice: "Perhaps, Angel, eet is trick, making thees thing too easy. Thees Millerick ees great *gringo*. Ees no fool, these . . ."

Her lip curled. "Were you mothered on sheep's milk, Pancho?"

"But eet is bes' to come back with few steers and safely . . ." She jerked the *cuerda*, and he stopped. Then in an even more whining voice than before: "I mean no offense, *Señorita* Angel. Eet is that I have family. Pray *Dios* I return alive. Pray *Dios*!"

Tucker hooked one leg to the saddle horn and grinned in his thin, off-center way, licking a cigarette into shape. "You better pray to *El Diablo*, Pancho, seein' the sort o' job we're on. Ain't you heard? Dead cattle raiders roast in hell."

"*Madre de Dios*." He whispered the words and crossed himself. Then to Tucker: "Fool. Ees no sin to steal from *gringo*."

"Be quiet!" The Angel said. She lifted her arm, pointing to the shadowy gash of Cañon Puerta. "Paraso, you and Chico will wait at the cañon mouth. It's there at the narrows that they'll give us trouble, if they're going to. If one of Millerick's cowboys opens fire, you will drive them to cover from above. Only be careful who you're shooting at, *sabe*?"

Paraso jerked back the head that was too large for his body and grinned, slapping the twin pistols at his hips. "So. Paraso knows the tricks of guns, my Angel."

She turned to the others: "The rest will ride in from the head of the cañon. Do all of you remember what I said back there?"

No one answered. An uneasy silence lay over the group, a silence broken only by the stamp of a fidgety mustang, the jerk and *jingle* of bit and bridle links, the *squeak* of saddle leather. She watched Paraso and Chico ride away and disappear over the lip of a shallow wash. Then, without saying more, she nudged the black and went on, riding with a little, silver *tinkle* of ornaments till the deep chasm of Cañon Puerta opened in front of them.

The moon was shining brighter now, rising above the distant summits of Sangre de Cristo, but its light did not reach inside Cañon Puerta, and served only to make it seem bottomless. The girl barely hesitated. She urged the black stallion forward and dropped from sight over the edge, finding a slanting ledge trail. It could be seen then that the cañon wall was not a single sheer drop but a series of steps where erosion had cut through successive strata of shale and sandstone. She worked her way slowly, time and again finding footing when there seemed to be nothing in front of her but sheer cliff and jagged talus slide. Behind her the men followed, cursing under their breaths from apprehension. At last the bottom was reached, and they worked across talus and thick thorn brush.

Beyond, now, the cañon floor was surprisingly flat and free of obstruction, a meadow enclosed by stone cliffs. A little streambed meandered back and forth, and there were some standing pools, or what had been pools before cattle churned it to thin mud. The herd was bedded down half a mile farther along.

"Look at 'em," Tucker said with a twist of his bitter mouth, the cigarette dead and scissored there as always. "Fat and peaceful and maybe their tails braided. By damn, they'll have some o' that taller run off 'em before tomorrow *siesta*. Only you were wrong about four hundred. There's eight hundred pulled in on that flat if there's a hoof."

"Then so much the better," The Angel snapped. "Come on!"

"¡*Señorita*!" A tall, big-beaked Mexican named

Santos wheeled his horse in front of her. "*Señorita* Angel has forgotten sometheeng! She has forgotten it is always best to scout ahead. Those *gringos* . . . I have fought them before. They are a breed of the devil. They are clever. Perhaps, as you think, they have only three or four cowboys as was true when they first brought these cattle here. But you have had no scout since dawn. Now perhaps many more. Perhaps . . ."

"Perhaps. You should have been a monk, and sure of tomorrow."

Her voice was low, barely audible to those in the outer fringe. Santos stood his ground, lips twisted down, his predatory eyes distended and hawk-like. "I do not wish to stumble into a trap."

"Were you raised on sheep's milk, too, Santos?"

"Hah!" He slapped his guns. "You have seen me, *señorita*. These guns. Notches for four men. Many times have I driven cattle when the moon was dark."

"Get out of my way!"

"No. You will make us stumble into a trap. So you will please to wait here while Miguel and myself ride three, four miles to the cañon narrows and . . ."

"You will help us drive the cattle as we have planned."

Her eyes had a dark fire through the slits of her mask, but Santos met them, held his horse as it was, blocking her, and swung around to appeal to

19

the others: "You will not let her take this foolish chance. Hear me, *caballeros*. . . ."

The girl's hand twisted without warning, sending the long-lashed *cuerda* unrolling. It seemed to pause an instant at full length. Santos spurred his horse and started to rake upwards with claw-like fingers, but he was too late. The lash struck, wrapped itself in successive coils around his neck. A half-choked scream ripped across his vocal cords. His horse lunged, and that, combined with the quick, backward snap of the girl's body, dragged him from the saddle.

He struck ground on one hip with leg doubled beneath him. His fingers were tearing at the whip, but for a second or two the girl held him against the tautness of it. Then she relaxed and the lash unwound.

Santos seemed to be stunned. He remained on the ground, head flung back, one hand propped behind him. The other hand was somewhat hidden. It moved slowly, then suddenly dragged at the Colt revolver he wore on his right hip.

"No, Santos." It was her voice.

The sound of it was hushed, yet something about it congealed his movement. The girl had swung herself around, and the long-barreled revolver, still holstered, was aimed down at him.

For seconds the scene was frozen in that manner with Santos's distended eyes fastened on the gun muzzle. He made a dry gulp that rolled his pointed

Adam's apple up and down. His lips moved and a dry whisper came out: "Eef you pull trigger, Angel, it will be warning to *gringos* and no steers we will drive tonight."

"And so you remain among the living. Get up."

Miguel caught the pony and led it back. He was a flat-faced fellow, this Miguel. Apparently not too bright, and used to taking orders from Santos. Santos got the bridle from him, and then took time to brush off his fancy foxed pants. They were not the pants of an ordinary *bandido*. Santos had taken them from the body of a general of La Republica the summer before and had guarded them more carefully than his own life ever since.

The soft drawl of Tucker, the *gringo*, came with a laugh in it. "Now that makes two of us, Santos. You and me. Only I learned my lesson. She showed me who was boss. But I reckon you're only coiled like a rattler in the sagebrush."

"What do you mean by that, *Señor* Gringo?" Santos spat the question as he mounted, bringing his pony around with a brutal twist.

"Meant just what I said. I know your kind, Santos. Any man that would wear pants off a dead man . . ."

"You've talked too much, both of you. I thought I was leading *bandidos*, not a flock of chattering magpies. I brought you to raid cattle and win gold for your pockets. You all know what to do!"

She rode ahead, swinging the *cuerda*, whipping

the first of the longhorns up and into motion.

They were well-fed cattle, but still wild as buffalo after having spent their lives in the brush country. There was no trouble moving them. Some of them set off at a lope, and the running of those started the others. Their hoofs became louder as the whole herd got in motion; it rose as thunder held in by cañon walls. More light here as the walls widened and moon reflected down, but dust was rising, blanking things out. *Bandidos* riding directly in the herd's drag tied handkerchiefs across their nostrils as the drive went on.

Ahead of them were the narrow cañon portals where the walls closed in like twin pillars, and in the distance a rocky plain made milk-white by the moon. Still no sound of alarm, although those three cowboys camped at the cañon mouth must have heard the drive by now.

The Angel, pushing her stallion hard, got ahead of the others, riding a ledge trail somewhat above the dust and bellow. She could see the first cattle just moving through the narrows. No cowboys trying to stop them. There was a chance the camp had been made at Esmeralda Springs, two miles away, but still there should be someone, a single man on watch, trying to turn the lead steers with the shots of his six-shooter.

Most of the cattle had thundered through the narrows. Only stragglers were left. Two *bandidos* spurred as close as they could, knowing there must be no delay in turning the herd toward the Río.

A gunshot knifed the dark. She could see the powder flash from high among the rocks. In another second, flame spurted from twenty places on both sides of the portals, centering on the two *bandidos* in the lead. Range was short, but dust, darkness, and swift movement gave them a chance to escape.

The girl's voice rose in command, its shrillness cutting through the hammer of gunfire. She was ordering her men to retreat upcañon. Those guns placed at the narrows made it the mouth of death.

A man cried in pain. He was hit. Here and there an answering shot came from the cañon as one of the *bandidos* fired a blind shot back at the ambush.

The Angel watched her men turn and head back upcañon. Her lips were pulled back, showing grim satisfaction in one thing—that the first shot had come too soon, saving her men from extermination.

She swung her horse around, reached to the scabbard beneath the saddle, drew out the lever-action Winchester. There was a cartridge in the barrel. She worked the lever a trifle to make sure, saw the brassy cartridge glint, closed the action again. Her stallion seemed to know what was expected of him, and found his way down rock, guided by the slight pressure of her knees.

Others were on the run, and the cool satisfaction that lay on her face showed it was what she wanted. Then her lips drew tightly as she saw old Esteban, her lieutenant, ride past, holding with both hands to the pommel, one side of his shirt turning dark from blood.

"Esteban." There was a new tone in her voice, one she seldom let anyone hear. It was soft, with a womanly warmth.

"Notheeng!" he hissed. "Only the scratch. How many time has Esteban been hit worse. Weeth El Capitán Buvaro in the revolution. Now we must ride, my Angel."

"Where's Nuñez?"

"Nuñez . . . dead."

"Someone informed on us, Esteban."

"*Sí*. Someone. But we must not die here."

The ambushers were clambering down from the portal rocks, leading horses from concealment. The Angel came close to old Esteban, hooked his belt over the saddle horn.

"Ride ahead!"

"But *señorita* . . ."

She swung her *cuerda*, sending Esteban's horse away at a gallop with the old *bandido* bent over, clinging on. Back at the narrows someone was shouting, cursing because the ambush had failed. It was a womanish voice, and his shouting made it sound more womanish than ever.

# II

Sound of the man's voice did something to The Angel's expression, making it thin-lipped, making her hands tighten on the Winchester. She recognized it as Millerick's—boss of the Block M.

For a few seconds she sat without moving, watching the shadowy forms of men moving down and across rocks, their guns making an occasional metallic glint in the moonlight. The first of them mounted, rode into the open. He caught sight of old Esteban who was clinging to his horse, riding up the cañon. The man tossed a rifle to his shoulder, hesitated to aim, but The Angel's Winchester came to life and its slug smashed him sidewise.

He clung for a moment, then pitched off, one boot higher than his head. The horse was charging at a startled gallop, and for a second the man's other boot hung up in the stirrup, but it came free and he had strength and presence of mind to scramble for cover.

The Angel's bullet had been wholly unexpected. It sent the ambushers scrambling back to cover. Shots laced the night once more, but they were firing at the memory of her gun flash. Most of them were wild, but one fanned close, and another sent spatters of lead as it glanced from a rock in

25

front of her horse's hoofs. The *whine* of bullets seemed to act on her like wine, making her lips grow more full, her nostrils flare slightly.

From above two other guns were firing. That was Paraso and little Chico. She waited, gun ready, showing no inclination to fight blindly. Fifteen or twenty seconds went by with Millerick's shouting in his womanish treble, most of his words unintelligible amid shooting, but the last sentence clear enough to make a smile twist down the corners of her mouth. "I never saw a hired killer yet that wasn't snake-belly yellow inside!" he screamed at them.

A man came into moonlight, crawling across stones. She tossed the Winchester to her shoulder, pressing the trigger at the same instant. It was close enough to send him wriggling away like a Gila monster.

She nudged the horse away, anticipating the returning volley. Millerick was screaming at them, uttering a stream of abuse, ordering them to their horses. Finally the ringing sounds of steel-shod hoofs on stone told her they were obeying.

She kept the stallion moving across stones, through shoulder-high brush. Her *bandidos* were far away now. No sound of their running horses. Even Esteban would be on his way up one of the narrow ledge trails.

There's something about the feel of a horse beneath a man that gives him courage, and the

26

ambushers were on their way, first five of them in a tight galloping knot, then four more, and the others strung out behind. She was close enough, and the moon was bright enough—she could have dropped one or two, but there was no point in that. She kept going, the stallion taking it easy, his rawhide-shod hoofs making scarcely a sound on slab rock when he crossed it.

Millerick's high-pitched voice came from an unexpected place in the dark. She reined in to listen. He was still shouting orders to his men. Rage at his failure seemed to have rendered him hysterical. He stopped abruptly, and the girl could tell he was listening to someone who had ridden up and was speaking with a drawl.

"What the hell?" Millerick screamed. "Talk up, man!"

The drawling voice was louder then, and she could hear the words: "I said you were a damned fool for ragging their tails upcañon. It's what they want you to do."

"Don't tell me I'm a fool!" he raged back. "One of you damned, cocky Texas Rangers always knows more about a rancher's business than he knows about it himself. If I'd listened to you, they'd probably have got off with every hoof of stock in this bunch and be halfway to the Río by now."

The Ranger's voice was still controlled, but there was a brittle substance to it: "If you'd

27

listened to me, Millerick, I'd have had the ringleader of these *bandidos* by this time. That's the one you want. Damn it, you can't kill every *bandido* in Chihuahua. There are more *bandidos* in Chihuahua than there are snakes."

"Then what would you have me do, go home?"

"No. Bring your men back through the portal. Those *bandidos* always start out with a plan. If shooting starts, they scatter, and it's every bushwhacking son of 'em for himself. But they always agree to rendezvous somewhere, and, if we can pick up the trail of just one of them . . ."

"No. I'll trap them all. Here, at the head of this cañon, and blast them down like cornered wolves."

"Want to bet?"

"Damn it, get out of my way."

"I *am* out of your way, seh," he answered with something like a laugh in his soft, Southern voice.

She had heard them plainly, every word, every inflection of voice coming across the night that suddenly seemed to have crystal silence after the thunder of hoofs and crash of rifle fire.

Millerick wheeled his horse and went past at a gallop. She'd been holding her stallion on a tight rein; now she nudged him on, covering a slow 100 yards along the cañon brush. Huge sandstone blocks had fallen from above, blocking the way, and she had to swing far out in avoiding them.

28

Gunfire was ringing from up the cañon, each shot sounding like a dozen as it bounded from the rock walls. Now and then her eyes caught flashes high above along the ledge trail. The rifle echo prevented her from detecting the Ranger's approach, and it was the stallion that gave her warning. He made a twitch, a sideward movement. She twisted in the saddle. Her Winchester still in her hands. She swung it, detecting the shadow of the horseman that had apparently materialized from nowhere.

He was close, so close that the rising moon, slanting down between the walls, gave an instant impression of his face. Young, lean, his hat tilted back in the typical cowboy angle. His six-shooter was drawn, but for the second he held it with barrel angled toward the sky.

Her spurs dug, sending the stallion on a charge through shoulder-deep brush. She pulled the Winchester's trigger, with its report and the report of the Ranger's six-gun coming on the same instant. The Colt was wild, a startled response, but she'd had slightly more time and the Winchester hammered, connecting, giving back ringing sound. It had struck his saddle horn, carving through leather and glancing off the steel core.

The Ranger rode a chestnut horse, larger and more high-blooded than the mustangs which were common as Sam Colt's pistols in that border country, so instead of starting out on a sunfishing lope as the average mustang would, the chestnut reared back and spilled his rider over and to one side.

He struck ground, twisted over, and over again, the bounding impact of his body seeming to explode the gun in his hand, the horse between them for a couple of seconds. It was the horse rather than his blind bullets that saved him. Then he was momentarily in the open, a rock just beyond. He plunged for it.

That was the instant. The Winchester was leveled, but for some reason she hesitated with memory of his face still in her mind. The Winchester pounded, sending a long streak of flame, but her hesitation had saved him, and he had disappeared, leaving only a white spot of bullet-burn atop the rock at the place where the center of his breast had been.

She spun away, giving the stallion his head, moving upcañon, still slow going, pounding brush. He was gone from beyond the rock and from the next. No telling where he was now. He was clever, escaping like that, so quickly despite moonlight and lack of brush cover. His horse was behind her, crashing brush. She knew then. He was there, capturing the animal. He'd be mounted in a moment, trying to overtake her.

She swung her horse through brush cover, lashed him to a run as she struck the cañon floor. She'd been right about the Ranger. He'd been retaking his rangy chestnut horse. He fired once, the bullet roaring past her ear. Again. The slug tore dirt from the stallion's thundering hoofs. There was a trail descending to a streambed and up the other side. She turned in the saddle, saw him galloping after her.

The chase was doing something to her, bringing a new expression to her face, acting on her like the shooting had acted a while before. The rush of wind, the gallop of hoofs, the *whine* of bullets fired at the crest of action—they were all things that appealed to her wild nature. Her lips were parted, smiling. Her hand went up, pulling off the black leather mask. She looked younger then, almost girlish.

There were two or three miles of the grassy cañon bottom, but beyond that were Millerick's hired *gringo* killers, swarming like ants from an overturned hill. She kept going. It was no longer necessary to urge the horse. In spite of the journey up from the Río Grande the animal was anxious for his chance to stretch his powerful legs. She leaned forward, speaking softly in his ear, turning her head each few seconds to keep watch on the Ranger behind. The distance between them grew and diminished, grew again. For the moment at least their horses were on a par.

Once more a steep descent to a streambed. She let shadows cover her, then reared back on the reins, bringing the stallion on haunches in a sliding stop. She turned, followed the streambed, arched over by desert willow, reached the cañon wall, commenced skirting it in the cover of manzanita. There was a steep pitch across dirt and slide rock, a ledge one could follow for twenty yards. No concealment there. Down below she could see the Ranger swinging his horse around.

He still did not see her, so she drew in for a second, lifting her two hands high, *cuerda* in one, Winchester in the other, and her voice rose in a high, jeering cry. Her voice could have been man's or woman's. He glimpsed her then, and wheeled to follow.

She spurred on and was hidden by more manzanita. The ledge played out. Another shelf of rock lay beyond. She quirted the stallion as he seemed to falter, and the big animal plunged on, pawing crumbling shale as he sought footing, and reached the ledge.

She caught another glimpse of the Ranger below. He was now hard in pursuit, and was dragging his Winchester from the scabbard. He didn't fire.

Up a bank, half rock, where sword cactus grew. The stallion had slowed, but was driving powerfully, climbing the slope. She smiled a little, knowing that such ground gave her the real advantage over ordinary horses. The stallion came from Spanish blood lines, but he was native to the hills of Chihuahua, and time and again she'd seen him run an ordinary animal half dead.

Behind her the Ranger's chestnut was driving, too. Coming faster than she'd expected. Only momentary glimpses of them down there, but her ear could tell. The Ranger's horse was shod with steel, while her own wore protecting coverings of rawhide that had been heat-shrunken to his hoofs.

A deep gully sliced down through the cañon. She descended into it by a zigzag trail, plunged deep into the manzanita at its bottom, slid off, and clapped her hat over the stallion's nostrils. He fought the black sombrero for an instant, trying to rear on hind legs, but she twisted him down with a strength no one would have suspected in her slim body.

The Ranger was already riding down from above. He loomed suddenly, a dark shadow against night sky. So close at that instant she could hear the labored breathing of his horse, the little *tinkle* of spur chains. He hesitated, swinging around, looking for her. A trail led back up the same side they had descended—apparently the only trail out. He took it, and after a minute the girl remounted and commenced groping along the other side. No trail worthy of the name—only a track such as panthers and wolves make, then it joined with another, and another until a fairly defined game trail pointed upward. The gorge forked, putting distance between her and the Ranger. They were a quarter mile apart at the crest.

She waited for him to appear and lifted her sombrero high in farewell before setting off at an easy canter toward Mexico across the Río Grande.

# III

The Angel forded the Río and headed across flat-rising mesa country to the vast dry cut called Río Jacinto. This was *bandido* country where even the wild-riding *caballería* feared to go in numbers less than a dozen, but she entered with the ease of long habit, finding her way without trouble through tumbled rock masses, across minor arroyos. She chose a cañon apparently no different than fifty others and followed the crooked V of its bottom for a half mile or so.

Someone moved, spoke, punctuating his word with the *click* of a gun hammer. Then he exhaled and spoke: "Ah! The Angel. We thought perhaps you had been killed."

"You would be such a fool!" She'd replaced her mask on crossing the Río, and beneath it her lips were barely smiling. "Who is it? Ricardo?"

"*Sí*. Ricardo." He was a skinny, ragged *bandido*, horribly scarred from an old bout with the *caballería* who had taken him, stood him against a wall at Mission San Juan de Camerónes, and shot him. They'd left him for dead, but there he was, six years later, still alive with one side of his jaw shot away.

"The others here?"

"Some of them, *señorita*."

"Esteban?"

"He is here."

"Wounded badly?"

"The ribs at his left side. A scratch to one like me who do not die even before guns of *caballería*. Paraso burned it out and made him to sleep."

She jerked her head, preventing any relief from showing in the cold austerity of her features. "Who has not come back?"

"Nuñez. . . ."

"Killed. Who else?"

"Zuninga. And Rojas."

"The others inside?"

"Yes, Angel."

She rode on, rounding a sharp cañon turn that brought her almost atop a small corral of gnarled mesquite trunks set in rocky ground and lashed together with iron-tough wrappings of shrunken rawhide. There were horses in the corral, a dozen or so. Beyond was a sort of cave hut made by roofing a natural crevasse with timber and flat slabs of shale.

A fire had been built a half dozen strides in front of the cave doorway, and now it was burning down to coals. She could see men and the shine of their rifles as she rode up and dismounted. Something about the uncomfortable silence told her that they'd been talking about her.

"So you lived!" It was Santos's voice.

"I always live." She located him. He was seated on the ground, cross-legged, peering at her with his protruding eyeballs. There was an octagonal-barreled .44 rifle lying across his knees. His grimy hand moved down and closed on the action, and maybe he'd have tried to use it if anyone except the dull-witted Manuel had been there to back him.

Some sticks of mesquite lay beside the fire, and her little, pointed boot swung, sending them into the coals. They flamed up with quick light, making all the men plainly visible. Santos's fingers moved to his throat, touching the red-raw streaks the girl's *cuerda* had left. He winced, peeling lips back from yellowish teeth. They were crooked teeth, with one in front grown over the other, and they gave him a pointed, coyote appearance.

He said: "Do not look at me like that, *Señorita* Angel. It is not my fault the raid went wrong. God be my judge, did I not offer to risk my life at scouting those *gringos*, and the life of my poor Miguel, too? And what did I get for my pains but . . . ?"

"You offered to." There was something in her tone that gave the words a deadly significance.

"But when the shooting started, where were you and your Miguel then? I saw everyone caught in *gringo* bullets except you and Miguel."

"You mean by that . . . ?"

"I'm talking, Santos. Perhaps when I'm through, you will get your chance."

That word "perhaps" made his face turn hollow from fear. He crouched forward, right hand closed on the rifle. She looked down on him contemptuously, and turned her gaze on Miguel. She spoke his name, and Miguel crept forward, dog-like, eyes shifting from Santos to the girl. Until that night Santos had been his god, but he'd seen that god lashed to earth by the girl, he'd seen him cringing then, and cringing now. It had left his poor mind bewildered.

"*Sí*," he whispered.

"Last night, Miguel, you came to the rendezvous drunk. Drunk on whiskey that is not cheap. There was oil on your hair, and a barber had shaved you. Powder and perfume were on the breast of your *chamarra*. Perfume of the girls from Casa Burdel in Lagunas. Is not that all so, Miguel?"

He shifted his eyes to Santos and back again. His mouth sagged open. He nodded and said: "*Sí*."

"That all cost a great deal of money, Miguel. Yet you have begged like a crippled blind man near the mission for two weeks past."

He peered up, eyes glistening through oiled hair that had fallen from beneath his sombrero.

37

"Where did you get the money?"

He was thinking, and his mind, in desperation, had an animal cleverness. But he thought too long, and it was obvious that any answer, no matter how reasonable, would be a lie. "I found it, *señorita. Sí* . . . found it." He clasped his hands. "*Madre de Dios*, judge your poor Miguel. Look down and be my judge. I found it. *El doblón de oro*. That I found. *El doblón*. Amid the rubbish where the Casa Durango burned three years ago."

"Where did you change this *doblón de oro*?"

"In the *burdel*. Forgive me for saying the word, *señorita*, but I am man who . . ."

"You have a purse in your pocket."

Miguel crouched forward, his frightened eyes glistening.

She raised her voice: "*La bolsa* . . . open it!"

He fumbled for the purse, drew it out. His thick fingers trembled at the drawstrings. He opened it and upended it in the dirt. Coins trickled and rolled, heavy silver, *pesos* following crooked paths across the ground. No one needed to count them to see that their value was greater than a single *doblón de oro*.

"You did well with your *doblón* to receive so much change. Did the barber pay you to put oil on your hair, and those girls of the Casa Burdel drop money in your pocket so they might rub powder from their cheeks across your *chamarra*?"

Her voice was low, heavy with contempt. Then suddenly it raised and lashed out: "Where did you get the money?"

"I found it, *señorita*. I found it. As I live . . . oh, *spiritus sanctus* . . ."

"Don't befoul the words of the Holy Mass with your lying tongue!"

"*Señorita*, listen. Hear me. Did I say I had found one *doblón de oro*? Oh, ha! Not one. Two *doblóns* it was. I had forgotten. Two *doblóns*. Behold. I was pawing through the rubbish, see, like this? . . . and suddenly there was a box. A box for *cigarros*. I opened it . . ."

The *cuerda* had been rolled in the girl's hand. It shot out suddenly and came to a stop with a report like a pistol's explosion. The lash did not touch him, but it left a dustless spot on the earth between his hands.

"Tell me true!" she cried.

"*Sí, señorita*. Yes, I will tell true. I was lying. I did not find it. It was given to me. I did not mean to do wrong in taking it. I did not . . ."

"Who gave it to you?"

He opened his lips to answer, hesitated. Men crouched forward to hear his words. His lips started to move. A gun tore silence with flame and explosion. The bullet struck Miguel in the back of the head, smashing him forward where he lay face down, his oiled hair mixing with dust. He trembled a single time, and lay still.

Santos crouched forward, the .44-caliber rifle in his hands. A wisp of smoke drifted up from the barrel.

The girl had flung herself to one side. Santos was halfway to his feet, still crouched. The fire was blazing, and for the second he could not see her over it.

She'd gone to one knee. It brought her side around with the Colt revolver swinging up. Her fingers found the trigger. Flame lashed from the cut-away bottom of the holster. The slug smashed the rifle from Santos's hands, the bullet glancing, following the bone of his forearm and emerging again to glance with a sharp *whine* from the rocks of the cañon beyond.

Shock of the bullet sent Santos spinning backward. Momentarily he was out of sight. She sprang across the fire, glimpsed him dragging himself to an upright position. She stood, hand still on the butt of the gun, its barrel aimed. He saw it and cringed, pushing himself back without rising, his wounded right hand leaving bloody prints on the bare, white earth.

"No. No, *Señorita* Angel. Do not shoot. Me . . . Santos . . . I who would risk my life for you. I am not traitor. Eet was just that the fool would have lied. He was jealous of me. Hated me. That foolish Miguel. He would say I hired him to be traitor. He would say that, *señorita*, and so I . . ."

"You killed him before he could tell where he

got the money. Before he could tell that, you gave it to him. And now, Santos, who was it gave the money to you?"

"No. I was angry, and so I killed him. Because . . ."

"Millerick gave you the money so you would lead us into the ambush. That's why you wanted to scout ahead. So you could get out of danger. So you could tell them where we were."

"No. I swear. . . ."

"You have another gun, Santos. The Colt at your hip. See me. See my hands are at my sides. You will get a chance. A chance you did not give that foolish Miguel."

"No." He shook his head. Fear had turned his face into something repulsive, made his cheeks seem hollow, his complexion grayish. His mouth was open, and a glisten of saliva showed at the corners. He kept shaking his head, saying—"No! No!"—forcing himself back.

She cried: "Draw your gun!"

She stood with tiny boots planted widely, hands at her sides, pistol still holstered. The firelight, coming from beneath, put her face in a new light, making it look white in contrast with the black leather mask.

He whispered: "No, *señorita*. You no shoot me . . . Santos . . ."

Her shoulder moved, and there was a slight swing of her supple body. That was all. It took

41

only a fragment of time—a fragment shattered by the explosion of the gun at her waist.

As always, she had simply angled it without drawing and fired through the open bottom of the holster. Santos thought he was going to die, but she had simply placed the second slug through his left wrist, leaving the hand shattered and dangling. He screamed and rolled over, over again, again, ending against the steep rocks beside the cave house. He tried to reach behind, but his hands were useless.

Her voice: "I will trust you now, Santos. For the moment." She jerked her head toward the corral. "Paraso! Saddle the traitor's horse."

Tucker's drawling voice came from the shadows: "You better pull that trigger one more time, Angel. Once through the *cabeza*. That's where you shoot rattlesnakes. Through the *cabeza*."

She laughed. A lock of light brown hair had escaped her sombrero and she turned, tucking it back. "Would you then expect me to shoot all the snakes in Chihuahua, *Señor* Gringo? And if I did, how many here would breathe with the dawn tomorrow?" Miguel's money was still strewn on the earth. She nudged it with her toe. "Divide it! It is all our pay for tonight's long ride."

"But we will ride again?" cried Paraso.

"Always we will ride again."

# IV

Tom Garrett, Texas Ranger, hooked one knee over the saddle horn and swore softly to himself. There was a touch of admiration in his voice. It wasn't often one saw a *bandido* in the grand style, and this one, to make things better, was obviously a girl. He had just reached the crest above Cañon Puerta. There he had expected to see his *bandido* on the lope across mesa land ahead of him. Instead, like an optical illusion, the *bandido* had appeared in another direction with a next to impassable gorge between them. To make it worse, the gorge had forked and he would have his choice of going back, or of riding miles out of his way in reaching the Río Grande.

So Tom Garrett laughed to himself, took time to roll and light a cigarette. Yes, it was a girl, all right. There was something in her motion as she waved to him. It had not been a man's gesture. Too supple at the waist, her shoulders too limber, body blending with the high fling of her arm. Garrett watched, dragging, inhaling the cigarette, as she rode out of sight across a curve of the country.

Garrett was young, too young for the lines that were stamped at the corners of his mouth, or for the narrowed hardness of his eyes. He was twenty-four and looked thirty. His face was tanned the hue of Apache moccasin, slightly darker than his sandy-bleached hair. He was lean, as though dehydrated, and turned to whip leather by the arid climate; there was a sinuous, Indian-bow resilience in his movements. At his waist, worn rather high after the style of men who spend much time in the saddle, was a Colt .44 revolver. A second pistol was carried as a spare in a latched-down saddle holster, and there was the Winchester in its scabbard beneath his right knee.

He seemed in no hurry to follow. He was no man to drive his horse beyond endurance. He finished the cigarette, rubbed the coal out against his bullet-scarred saddle horn before throwing it away. Then he rode at an easy jog across descending benches, turned west at the Río, and found the deep-punched hoof prints of the stallion filled with water. He swung down and hunkered on boot heels, looking at them. Río Grande water carried a yellowish silt that separated slowly, but this had cleared enough to show she was about a mile ahead.

He thought for a moment, narrowed eyes studying the Mexican side. It was always open season on Texas Rangers over there, and he had no authority except what he carried on his hip, but he mounted and crossed anyway, picking up her trail and losing it in the wind-swept rocks that stretched away toward the deep cleft of Río Jacinto.

He knew what the Jacinto was. Even when old Ramón Torretagles was lord of the country, when his armed *vaqueros* were riding *bandidos* into the ground, this Jacinto was the end of things. And it was worse now with Torretagles dead and his cattle empire reduced to a shell of its former grandeur.

He rode steadily, finding moon shadow against one wall of the Jacinto's wild cut. The bottoms were broad, sometimes three miles across with here and there small mesas and pillars of wind-carved rocks rising from the floor. There were side cañons, crooked and unexplored, every one of them a spot for ambush. Night breeze came coolly to his nostrils and with it the scent of a mesquite fire. He kept following it, losing it, finding it again as the breeze shifted unpredictably among the cañons. He drew up, eyes on a distant cliff. Movement. A single rider. Too far and too dark actually to see any detail, yet some slight mannerism told him it was the girl.

He started along a steep cañon, but swung back when he saw a fresh horse trail. There was another way, a path clinging to its steep side. He could see the fire then, some horse corrals, movement of men nearby. He kept going, and finally intercepted the main trail from the cañon bottom. Twice he saw the girl ahead of him.

The trail became steeper, a series of switchbacks; it followed a ledge across sheer, wind polished cliff. Sometimes its ledge was wide, as much as fifteen or twenty feet, then unexpectedly it would narrow and become barely sufficient for foothold with a horse's bulging side rubbing the cliff. He dismounted, led the chestnut, mounted again.

Now and then he paused to rest and look above, but he could see nothing—only the cliff wall rising and rising, ending in a ragged strip across the star-scattered sky. A rock rattled, struck a promontory, and roared air as it went past. He flattened himself, snubbing the chestnut close, blindfolding him with his hat. He did not know whether the rock had been rolled deliberately or not.

He went on. The trail seemed to last forever; actually it took no more than half an hour to reach the crest. She was riding across rim country miles away, still pushing the black stallion. He'd play hell ever catching that horse in a pure test of endurance.

He descended unmapped mesa and cañon toward a glint of lights that marked the little outlaw town of Lagunas. The lights seemed closer than they were, and morning was commencing to gray out the stars when he circled the live oaks that grew near Perpetuo Springs and rode between adobe houses down the town's one street.

Tom Garrett wore no bit of uniform or insignia that would mark him as an officer of Texas law, so he entered boldly as any *gringo* renegade with a price on his head, and paused in mid-street to water his horse at a masonry ditch that had been built a century before by Franciscan priests of the now ruined mission to irrigate the tiny orange groves below.

He looked around but no one came in sight except a ragged old peon, barefoot with a single rope suspender to hold his pants up.

"Help weeth your horse, *señor*?" he pleaded, taking off his straw hat and holding it in his hands. "For five *centavos* I will unsaddle your horse, *señor*."

Garrett flipped him an American 5¢ piece.

"Ah, *Don* Americano!" He rubbed the coin and touched his tongue to it, testing counterfeit, then thrust it somewhere in his ragged pants. He reached for the reins, but Garrett did not hand them over.

Instead, Garrett drew more small change from his pocket, spun another 5¢ piece through the air. "Tonight, I look for a black stallion."

The peon heard his words and backed away, eyes shifty: "I know no black stallion, *señor*."

Garrett spun him a third coin. "A black stallion."

"I do not know. I swear. . . ."

"Not for ten *centavos*?"

"Not for *el real*, not for *peso*. . . ."

Garrett's hand swung back, closing on the butt of his .44 pistol. He did not draw, merely lifted the gun a trifle in its holster. "The stallion," he said. "You saw it. Half an hour ago. A girl riding a stallion. Where did she go?"

The peon wanted to run, but the flat adobe fronts were like a wall making him face the *gringo*. He whispered: "*Nombre de Dios . . . no comprendo. . . .*"

"Tell me where she went."

"Perhaps to the corral of the *cantina*. The *cantina* of Pablo Alvaraz. But I know nothing. I am but poor. . . ."

"Sure. I never saw you before." Garrett tossed him the rest of the coins and walked away, leaving the peon whispering—"*Gracias.*"—and scooping them from the dirt.

Garrett walked on, leading his horse, crossed the hard-packed dirt that served as a sidewalk, keeping more or less in shadow as he approached some pole and adobe horse sheds behind the sprawling old *cantina*. From one of the larger buildings, a two-story affair of wood and adobe with iron grille work over the windows, came the pleasant, liquid sound of a guitar being played rapidly in fandango rhythm. A half dozen mustangs were tied to a rack nearby, so evidently their owners, *vaqueros* or *bandidos*, were making a night of it. No one seemed to be at the *cantina*, but a light was burning inside.

He tied his horse to a mesquite rail fence and climbed over it. The adobe horse shed stood beyond. He stood in the door for a moment, the stable odors seeming very strong after the long ride through chilly night air. A horse stamped and blew through nostrils, and he knew instinctively it was the stallion. There were other movements. A man spoke, cursing in Spanish.

Garrett walked inside across a dirt floor, soft and damp from hay and manure. There were stalls on one side only; on the other were some windows, like clefts through the thick adobe. Enough moonlight found its way to show him the general shape of the stable. He almost ran against the hostler who was just backing from a stall.

Garrett spoke to him in Spanish: "The girl's stallion . . . you cared for him, didn't you?"

"*Sí*, that creature of the devil."

"Where did she go?"

The hostler started to answer, checked himself. He was small, thin, and at first Garrett took him to be a boy. Reflected moonlight then showed him to be a skinny, narrow-faced fellow of peon stock with tiny, brass rings in his ears.

"Who are you?" the peon asked. "I do not know you, *señor*."

He started to back away, but Garrett's right hand shot out, catching him by the collar. He dragged the hostler around, rammed his back to a stall post. The fellow was quick and wiry, but his strength was no match for Garrett's.

"Where is she?"

"I don' know, *señor*. Me only poor stable boy. Me only . . ."

"Who is she?"

"How would I know? They tell me nothing. Me poor stable . . ."

"How long since she left?"

"Not long."

He let the man go. He asked: "This stable . . . whose is it?"

A voice came from the darkness behind him: "It is mine, *Señor* Gringo!"

Garrett spun around and saw the man's shape take form in the darkness. He was a large man, middle-aged, and too heavy, judging from the way he wheezed through nostrils from the effort of walking. He walked close, and the combination of native garlic and tequila on his breath was not pleasant.

The man said: "That is your horse tied to my fence?"

"Yes."

"Juan, you will get the *hombre*'s horse."

The hostler moved away, almost running to get through the door, but pausing just outside to peer back at them.

Garrett asked: "You own the *cantina*?"

"*Sí*."

"You are Pablo Alvaraz?"

"*Sí*, Pablo Alvaraz. But I have not had the pleasure . . ."

"My name is Smith. John Smith."

"Here all *gringos* are named John Smith."

"There is a stallion here. A black stallion ridden in tonight. I want to buy him."

"Ho, ho! You would buy the black stallion?" He stopped laughing and spoke in a harsh, low voice: "You are being a fool. The horse is not for sale."

"Everything is for sale."

"So *gringos* believe, but this time you are wrong. Believe me, *señor*, the stallion is not for sale."

"Let me talk to his owner."

"The owner is not here."

"Where can I find him?"

"Perhaps at the *casa* of *Señora* Jamaica."

"What is his name?"

"It is . . . I believe . . . Juan Smith."

"I'm not joking, Alvaraz." He took a step, and Alvaraz fell back. It was dark, but for the moment Garrett could see him silhouetted against the moonlit doorway. He went on, voice low but with an intense note in it: "You're not fooling me. I know the stallion does not belong to a man, but a woman. She rode in here not half an hour ago. Where is she?"

Alvaraz muttered a word or two through his teeth. There was a pistol thrust in a sash at his waist. Not a revolver. It was one of those old percussion cap affairs, double-barreled, loaded with buckshot. It was heavy and slow to get into action, but capable of turning a man's belly inside out if it struck.

"Where is she?" Garrett hissed. "The woman. I followed her here."

Alvarez knew he was silhouetted against the doorway. He turned, tried to lose himself in the shadow of an empty stall. Garrett knew his hand was swinging for the double-barreled pistol.

Garrett took a long stride, the .44 drawn from his holster. He hesitated an instant and brought the barrel down, catching him across the wrist. The double pistol *thudded* to the earthen floor.

Alvaraz gasped from pain and went to one knee, holding his wrist. Garrett had an impression of his eyeballs, rolled up, focused on the gun. He staggered to his feet, retreated. The double gun lay at Garrett's feet. He booted it back.

"Take your gun. Put it in your *cinturón* and be damned sure to keep it there, *sabe*?"

"*Sí*," he breathed.

"Where is she?"

"In the *cantina*, *señor*. Waiting, at a side table."

"Who's she waiting for?"

"Perhaps for you."

Garrett laughed softly and moved through the door.

"Why yes. Maybe she is. *¿Quién sabe?*"

The *cantina* was an ancient building of adobe

and mountain pine, built in the form of a square with a patio in the center. Originally it had been *residencia* of one of the country's cattle barons, but now half of the building had been turned into granary, storehouse, and stable with only the big salon in use as a *cantina*. Garrett walked beneath the pole awning and looked inside.

The room was wide and low, its ceiling supported by dozens of fancy carved pillars, gilded once, but now tarnished from a generation of tobacco smoke. At one end was a bar with a bit of rusty mirror behind it. Overhead hung four candles in a suspension holder. They lighted the bar well enough, falling strongly on the head and shoulders of the sleeping bartender, but the light played out rapidly across the room and left far walls in almost complete darkness.

No one seemed to be there. Only the sleeping bartender. He walked around to the patio where a second door led inside. He saw her then, seated at a table near the far wall, a glass of red wine in front of her.

He stood for a moment, surprised by her youth and beauty. Her complexion was not dark as he had expected. Only the tan of desert sunshine. Her hair, where it could be seen beneath her silver-decorated sombrero, was light brown. The upper portion of her face seemed to be in deep shadow, then he saw it was not shadow but a black leather mask with slitted eyeholes.

No one but the girl and the sleeping bartender. He moved inside using the pillars for concealment and seated himself against the wall. Then he edged over a little and got a second view of her face. She did not turn. The wine still in front of her. She couldn't have more than sipped it. She was waiting for someone.

A quarter hour passed while dawn grew up across the barren hills, lighting the flat sides of adobe buildings but making the *cantina*'s interior seem darker than ever. From *Señora* Jamaica's he could hear the guitar being played in faster rhythm, a tarantella with men's voices rising to accent it. One of the girls was evidently dancing on a table, and the whole affair would probably end in a knifing.

Hoofs struck the street with a sudden, galloping rattle. They came to a stop out front. There was a coarse babble of men's voices, the *jingle* of big-rowelled spurs. One of the voices dominated the others, and the girl seemed to recognize it. She sipped her wine and turned a trifle in her chair, hitching herself a little so the long-barreled pistol at her waist swung freely.

She was ready, watching the door when they *clomped* in. Three of them. Rough renegades of the border. Their leader was a massive fellow, so huge across stomach and shoulders that his legs looked out of proportion, spindling and bowed. His face was flat and massive, thick-featured, oily and dark. He had mustaches so long he'd tied them beneath his chin with a scrap of red ribbon, giving him an appearance that was at once preposterous and sinister. His huge hands gleamed with gold and silver rings, and there were gold rings in his ears, too. His trousers, dirty and drooping, had been costly items once, cream and brown with gold braid down each leg. Around his waist hung two belts heavy with cartridges and holstered six-shooters. He carried a knife partly concealed in a sheath at the back of his neck. Across his arm was a carbine repeating rifle. The total weight of guns, knives, and cartridges must have been twenty pounds, but he swaggered under the load with the carelessness of long habit. His companions were less spectacular in appearance. Simply more of the rough renegades of the border.

The huge man stalked across the room, noticing neither Garrett nor the girl. The bartender awoke and was blinking, trying to get his wits about him. The huge man paused for a second or two, waiting, and, when the bartender made no move to get up, he reached with a gorilla arm, seized him, lifted him by the back of his velvet and braid jacket, and held him with toes barely touching the floor.

"Ho. You would sleep when El Gallo come to your miserable *cantina*?" He roared the words, apparently pleased at this opportunity of showing his strength. He let the bartender back to his feet but did not release him. Instead, he leaned farther than ever, and jerked him back and forth, slamming him alternately to the bar and backbar: "Wake! You hear? Wake! Wake! Thees is El Gallo come to wake you up. Is not enough time to sleep in the grave? Men do not sleep when El Gallo come. You hear? Men drink, men dance, men have beautiful women when El Gallo come ride to town." He paused, breathing hard through nostrils and held the poor bartender at arm's length, then with massive strength he flung him, sprawling, to the floor. "Is it not so?" he roared to his companions.

His companions accepted the display in a spirit of high humor, shouting laughter and beating fists on the bar.

"So!" El Gallo wheezed in the manner of a task well done. He took off his sombrero, wiped dust and perspiration away. "Tequila," he muttered. The bartender was just picking himself up from the floor. "You hear me, jackass? Tequila for El Gallo to cut the dust of alkali from his throat. Tequila for the men of El Gallo, his brave Tito and Rojas."

El Gallo. The name fit him. He bore a certain resemblance to a gamecock with his diminutive legs, his huge trunk and shoulders, his habit of standing erect with shoulders flung back. Everyone in the border country had heard of him—a *bandido* who from time to time broke the monotony of cattle raiding and highway robbery with a fling at revolution. He'd led a couple hundred brigands, killing and looting throughout the length of Chihuahua when Juárez was carried to power, but now the government of Mexico had a price on his head.

El Gallo tossed down a huge drink of tequila, wiped thick lips on the back of his hand, and turned, hitching the weight of guns and cartridge belts. His eyes roved the *cantina*. He spat.

"Notheeng here! No girls, no music. Only these four candles for light." He jerked his head around and said to the bartender: "Where is that swine, Alvaraz? Go. Tell him he has El Gallo for guest. Tell him this. Tell him El Gallo would have lights, music, and women while he rests an hour or two." He laughed with a twist of thick lips, and added: "While he waits for that woman, Hija de Satanás."

He hadn't seen the girl, and the sound of her brittle voice made him straighten suddenly.

"You are talking of me, *bandido*?" she asked.

El Gallo recovered himself. He grinned, showing yellowish, broken teeth. In grinning, his lower jaw pulled the tied mustaches tight, making his face look grotesque. "Ha! So you are here so queek, *señorita*. . . ."

"There was a name you called me."

# V

Garrett slid back in his chair, a movement that freed his pistol. He had no immediate intention of drawing or of disclosing his presence. It merely made him feel better to be ready. He simply sat, tilted a trifle back in the chair, watching El Gallo and the girl.

The girl was still sitting, apparently the same posture, one hand on the table, the other in her lap. Her lips were drawn thin, the corners of her mouth twisted down showing her contempt for the *bandido* chief.

El Gallo chortled deeply in his heavy throat. The laugh grew. He placed hands on hips, spread his feet widely, tilted his head back. "Ho, ho! So you hear! I call you thees that you are called behind your back. The daughter of Satan. So. La Hija de . . ."

Her body barely moved, only a swing of her slim waist, a slight sideward movement of her right hand. The room was suddenly ripped by explosion. Flame lashed from beneath the table. The bullet tore dust and splinters from the floor, and for a second El Gallo was sent staggering.

He hadn't been wounded. The bullet had shattered his right boot heel. He roared something, stopped. One could tell by his expression that a thought was registering in his thick brain. He looked at her, standing sidewise on one high heel and one low, the grin slowly progressing across his massive face.

"You devil. You beautiful she-devil with gun. Ho, ho! Where else is such a devil with the gun as this woman waiting for me? This woman who waits El Gallo?"

He limped forward, paused across the table from her, hooked a chair with his boot toe, spun it around, and sat down, his weight creaking the chair. "So. It does not take *Señorita* Angel long to wet the bellies of *gringo* cattle in Río Grande mud! You have them here already to deliver El Gallo?"

"I have no cattle."

"So? You did not . . . ?"

"The *gringos* were warned I was coming. One of your traitor *bandidos*! Santos, who you trust so much."

"I trust no man," he growled. His face was reposed and ugly as he thought it over. He lifted massive shoulders, let them fall. "So. It sometime happen. You killed Santos, of course."

"I shot him through both hands."

"Then I will shoot him a third time when he comes to me. A third time. Through the brain." He shrugged again. "Ha, so. But you will raid again. Always *mañana*. It is too bad I cannot pay you the gold I bring. But El Gallo cannot pay gold without cattle. . . ."

"You will lend me a thousand *pesos*."

"Ho! You think perhaps El Gallo find thousand *pesos* in pockets of these men I sometimes stop on road to Ciudad Chihuahua? You think . . . ?"

"I need one thousand *pesos*. The cattle will be delivered to you next week."

He thought it over, massive forearms planted on the table, eyes on her face. His thick lips started to smile. "*Sí*. One thousand *pesos*. Gold. Perhaps, for *you,* one thousand *pesos, señorita*. Perhaps for *you* would El Gallo empty his purse and no *gringo* steer ever to sell back across border."

"The cattle will be delivered as I said. Next week. The thousand *pesos, Señor* Bandido!"

"One thousand *pesos* I have, as you know, but not in my pocket. This much moneys, it is very heavy. El Gallo would not want *señorita* to carry it alone. So he will help you. So?"

Her voice was brittle as broken glass. "I am tired of hearing you. I am tired of looking at your foolish face. I am tired of smelling your clothes filled with horse's sweat. Give me the thousand *pesos*."

"But you have ridden so far. Over Río, and more. And behold your poor Gallo. He, too. The many miles to meet you here. So it is good that you should sit with him, and you should have drink together." He gestured high, snapping fingers. "Wine, you hear, *Señor* Jackass? Your best Spanish wine for El Gallo and his *señorita*."

The bartender came on the run, trying to draw a cork from a bottle of Malaga wine. The cork had been driven hard, many years before in a winery of old Spain, and the corkscrew straightened leaving the cork as before. The bartender stood helplessly, looking with frightened eyes, first at the bottle, and then at El Gallo. The *bandido* chief cursed, seized the bottle, set it on the table, and shattered the neck with a blow of his six-shooter. He then poured two glasses full to the brim and lifted one in his thick fingers.

"To you. The Angel. To The Angel . . . the woman who is match for El Gallo!"

He had paid her the supreme compliment at his disposal, and now he waited, beaming, for her response. She lifted the glass, not to her lips, but level with her right ear. El Gallo suddenly knew that she was going to throw it, but he did not move. He sat as he had been, an expression of set truculence on his lips, and took the wine across the face.

Still no movement. No sign that he even felt the wine strike him. The stuff ran down his thick neck, staining his shirt, the front of his fancy braided military tunic.

"Ha!" He hissed the syllable. "You jaguar! You would spit in the face of El Diablo, no?"

"Give me the thousand *pesos*!"

"Of course. Even after this will El Gallo give you the thousand *pesos*. El Gallo will do this because he like spirit. In horse, even in man he shoot, does El Gallo like spirit." He leaned across, wine still gathering in big drops and falling from his chin. "But mostly of all does El Gallo like spirit in beautiful woman!"

"The *pesos*."

"Behold me, *Señorita* Angel." He struck his chest a blow with fist and forearm. "Behold this El Gallo of yours. El Gallo who ride for Juárez and La Republica. El Gallo who this traitor Juárez would now stand against wall and shoot. Two years ago did this Juárez send his *caballería* for to capture El Gallo, and then was El Gallo's men so few he must run like *lobo* to hide in cañons of Río Jacinto. Last year again came these *caballería*, but El Gallo did not run. He fought them from rock to rock, one . . . two days. Next year El Gallo will chase that coward *caballería* into Sonora. And so will all of Chihuahua be ruled by El Gallo. After that, who knows? Sonora and Coahuila. Durango. *Sí*. Behold now your Gallo. *Bandido* no longer, but rich, powerful weeth palace in Cuidad Chihuahua. Then will be El Gallo great, a *don*!" The word "*don*" pleased him and he beat on the table with forearm and fist, striking it so hard that dust rose from the floor. "*Don* Gallo! *Don* Gallo! Behold this great *Don* Gallo who no man dare say smell like sweat of horse." He stopped bellowing and leaned forward. "You see, thus will your Gallo be. He must then have woman great, like himself. He must have woman worthy of him who will sit at his table, in his great palace in Chihuahua. And this woman it will be you, *señorita*."

Her lips tried to form a word that would show her contempt. "You greasy peon! You pig!"

He watched her, face sagging from amazement. Apparently he had not expected a second rebuff. He licked his lips, glanced around at his men, the two *bandidos* at the bar. They had heard, and their hearing had wounded the prestige of El Gallo. He lunged to his feet. The girl saw him coming, and was up ahead of him. Her hand moved to the pistol butt, but his weight drove the table back, ramming her against the wall.

The gun exploded, lashing flame, leaving a light-colored scar on one of the pillars. He charged on. She tried to fire again. The table kept her from swinging the gun up in its swivel holster. She tried to draw it. He swung his arm, batted it away. The gun was gone, thumping across the darkened floor.

He seized her by the wrist, dragged her forward. For a moment she was against him, then with feline quickness she twisted away. Her hand came up, nails raking his cheek. They left streaks that were white for an instant, then red as they filled with blood.

He still held her with one hand, rubbed the other across his cheek, drew it away, and looked at the slick smear of blood. She stood still, panting through clenched teeth, then with a sharp movement bent down and away, and her wrist slipped from his fingers.

He started after her. A chair was in his way. He trod it underfoot, smashing it to splintered rungs.

"Ho! *Señorita* Jaguar! *Señorita* of the long claws. Sometime already has El Gallo tamed jaguar to lap milk and walk on string at his heels."

She moved back. The *cuerda* had been thrust in her sash. She drew it, swung it overhand. The lash unrolled quickly as a striking snake. El Gallo saw it, but he simply stood his ground, not wincing, letting it carve his cheek.

He stood with boots spread widely, hands on hips. The *cuerda* swung again, ripping a ragged hole through his uniform tunic. His thick lips twisted. He started to laugh. The sound grew from his throat and became a roar.

"Ho! Ho! Thees is woman for El Gallo! Thees is one they call Hija de Satanás not for notheeng!"

She swung, and the lash cut his face again.

"Oh, ho! Harder! Harder, you devil cat." He stamped his boots, raising dust from the ancient floor. She swung the whip again, again. Blood ran down his face, soaking the collar of his shirt. Then suddenly his laughter stopped. He took the *cuerda*'s lash one more time without wincing, then roared and charged forward.

He caught the whiplash on an outflung hand.

The girl tried to retrieve it, and swing its shot-loaded butt. No time. She made an effort to twist away along the wall, but El Gallo was over her.

He seized her wrists and forced them behind her. She twisted back and forth, teeth bared. It was like fighting against the strength of a great bear. El Gallo forced her arms together, got hold of both wrists in one hand, leaving his other free. He reached up, jerked her sombrero off. Her golden-brown hair was fastened down by a bit of mantilla lace. He pulled the mantilla off, and her own fruitless struggles made hair cascade in thick, waving masses over her slim shoulders.

Sight of the billowing hair did something to El Gallo. His eyes brightened, became triumphant and gloating in the midst of his broad, blood-smeared face. He was breathing hard through nostrils. Her dress was ripped. His hand came up, ripping it farther, revealing a slim, white shoulder.

"See? You should be woman. Like woman in ballroom gown, with hair on shoulder. So thus you would be at table of El Gallo."

He bent over, pressed his lips against the skin of her shoulder. She fought him, but his lips were still pressed, leaving a smear of his blood.

Tom Garrett was on his feet, crossing the room. The two *bandidos* saw him and shouted a warning. One of them went for his gun, stopped as Garrett's .44 came from its holster. El Gallo became aware of him. He jerked his head up, backed away, dragging the girl by her two wrists, his free hand swinging down for a gun.

Garrett could have killed him, but poor light and the struggling girl made it too great a chance. He sprang forward, vaulting the upset table. El Gallo's gun was free of its holster. It exploded, whipping lead and burning powder, but the girl had ruined his aim.

The wall was close and El Gallo did not notice. He struck it hard, rebounded, and Garrett smashed the pistol barrel down across his skull.

El Gallo's fingers relaxed, freeing the girl. He reeled forward, eyes rolled like the eyes of a beef under a slaughter pen mallet. He struck the floor on bent knees, groggy but not unconscious. He had a brute brain, impervious to ordinary degrees of punishment.

The girl saw her gun on the floor. A long-barreled Colt Army pistol. Garrett seized her arm and tried to force her toward the door, but she twisted away from him with a mountain cat's strength that took him by surprise.

"Get out of here!" he shouted.

"Leave me alone. I do not need your help. I need no man's help."

One of the *bandidos* was still at the bar, tense, hunched forward, hands on the legs of his trousers but lacking the guts to go for his guns while Garrett had the .44 angled in his direction. The other *bandido* was nowhere in sight.

Garrett took a step to one side—glimpsed him. A shine of gun metal. He knew the *bandido*'s gun was aimed at him. Explosion. It was the girl's pistol. She'd fired without turning, aiming across her waist, beneath an uplifted left arm.

The heavy slug struck, spinning the *bandido* halfway around. The gun dangled in his fingers as he stood with shoulders propped against the bar. Then, with a foolish, slack-jawed expression on his face, he slid to a sitting position with legs thrust straight out, his *peso*-rowelled spurs digging little grooves across the floor. He'd been hit in the side, and, whether it was a vital spot or not, the shocking power of that .44 would keep him down a while.

Crash of gunfire seemed to bring El Gallo around. He started fumbling his way to his feet, and stopped, looking up into the round muzzle of The Angel's gun. "The one thousand *pesos*!" she cried.

His heavy, bloody face twisted into sort of a smile. "Ho! Ho! What woman. What woman for El Gallo." He felt in his pockets, dug out a purse heavy with gold coins, and tossed it across the floor. "What woman for El Gallo's table when he is master of Chihuahua."

She thrust the purse in her sash. El Gallo was still on hands and knees. He was crawling toward her, still talking about being master of Chihuahua. She let him come on a few feet. Her finger squeezed the trigger, sending a bullet that tore splinters from the floor between El Gallo's hands.

"What woman for El Gallo . . ."

She backed away, the gun rocking again, again, smashing dust and splinters into his bloody face. At the door she hesitated to scan the room, then backed to the patio.

Garrett was there ahead of her. He walked with long strides to the patio's rear exit and waited there.

She did not see him in the deep shadow. He seized her wrist, swung her around.

"I don't blame El Gallo," he said. "I don't blame him a damned bit."

"I did not ask you to help me," she hissed. "Why did you not keep your gun in its holster?"

"Maybe I was jealous of El Gallo."

"Let me go!"

"I'd like to see you without that mask first."

Her head darted down, sharp teeth sinking into his wrist. Pain and surprise made him release her. Next instant she had leaped back, hand swinging the .44 on its swivel holster, its barrel aimed directly between his eyes.

"You're a thankful little witch, aren't you?" he asked.

"I thank no man. I hate all men!"

He watched her back away through the patio door, then turn and hurry to the adobe stable where her black stallion waited.

# VI

She rode away. Garrett made no attempt to follow. Instead, he rode north, skirting the grove of dwarf oranges below town, taking the old stage road down Lagunas Valley. By this route it was a long ride to the Río Grande, for the road swung east and back again, avoiding the Río Jacinto. He kept going until the sun of afternoon rebounded from barren, gray earth, striking his face like heat from a white-hot cook stove, and then hunted some mesquite shade and swung down to sit, Indian fashion, smoking one cigarette after another, looking across descending mesa and arroyo to the deep cut where the Río Grande made a streak of metallic reflection through rising heat waves.

He'd been there half an hour when the *clatter* of hoofs on stone warned him that someone was coming. He did not change position, merely remained cross-legged in the mesquite's half concealment, watching the rider's approach. It was El Gallo. Alone. The mustang he rode was slightly larger and heavier-legged than most, but El Gallo's size made him seem burro-small. The huge, pointed sombrero on his head, the *tapaderos* that almost brushed the grass, the serape over his shoulder, and all the load of guns and belts made the mustang seem even smaller.

El Gallo approached within 100 yards, and then

angled off, and in a quarter of an hour dropped over a bulge of the country.

Garrett spat out the sodden remnant of his cigarette, drew the latigo of his saddle tight, remounted, and took his time about following. He reached the bulge of country, but El Gallo was already lost from view. Tracks led around the face of a mesa, and down an arroyo trail.

The arroyo became progressively deeper, the bottom broadened a trifle, and Garrett drew up at sight of a corral and shack. Not a dwelling. Just an overnight shanty for *vaqueros* from the Torretagles ranch.

He dismounted, went on afoot, and finally he lay belly down across the hot dirt and stones of the arroyo side and peered down through parted cactus swords. He'd been closer to El Gallo than he thought. The *bandido* had dismounted and was turning his mustang loose in the tiny corral. There was a second horse in the enclosure, saddled. Someone was evidently waiting for him.

El Gallo dropped the corral bar once more in place and stalked, heavy and bowlegged, toward the shack. A canteen was hanging on a peg. He drank from it, hung it back, said something. His voice was a snarl. It was a voice to go with his face that by now had swollen to something scarcely resembling a man's.

An answer came from a man inside the shack, and whatever it was did not please El Gallo, for he roared: "Come out! Come out, you coward ass when El Gallo say!"

He hunched forward, hands resting on the butts of his pistols, watching while a skinny, narrow-faced Mexican appeared in the door.

The skinny one walked on into the sunlight, carrying himself sidewise after the manner of wounded men. One arm was supported by a sling fashioned from a black kerchief; the other was rolled in dirty rag bandages. Garrett knew then who he was—he was the Santos that The Angel had mentioned back in the *cantina*.

El Gallo was saying something to him, empha-sizing with bull-like shakes of his head. Flies were around, and they kept settling in the wounds of El Gallo's face, and he kept slapping them away. Only a few disconnected phrases came to Garrett across the heavy heat of afternoon.

Garrett slid back out of sight, climbed the arroyo side until the bulge of it let him stand upright, then he circled, and moved down directly toward the shack, sitting, digging boot heels into the steep slope, taking care not to dislodge a pebble or stream of dirt that would betray him.

The shanty roof came in view, but he kept going, clinging to the sheer slope, and at last found boot support and a measure of concealment behind some thorny mesquite. The shanty hid both men, but he could hear them plainly.

Santos was whining: "Heaven be my judge, I do

everytheeng as you say. But the shot. Someone fired too queeck from those narrows at the head of the cañon when damn' cattle . . ."

"You have failed. Hear me, Santos? You have failed, and your failing has made El Gallo one great fool."

"Behold my hands! Broken. Shot through . . . in your service. . . ."

"El Gallo does not like to be made the great fool. Tell me, jackass, how was it The Angel found out you were a traitor?"

"Not me. It was not my fault. Miguel! It was he and his *doblón de oro*."

"You showed her the gold I . . . ?"

"No. Miguel . . . he it was. . . ."

"And where is Miguel?"

"I killed him."

"So. You are then good for sometheeng. That is one El Gallo will not have to finish."

The import of the man's words struck Santos. He backed into sight, hands lifted above his face. "No. You would not. Listen to me! Hear what I say. . . ."

"Hah! Pah!" He spoke the syllables as he spat. "Tell me, jackass, how much more did you talk to The Angel?"

"I swear it, El Gallo. Notheeng. By the name of all the saints. They try to make me talk, with the fire tortures they try, but your brave Santos . . ."

"Show El Gallo the blisters of this fire

72

torture that you suffered, oh, brave jackass."

Santos's eyeballs looked sharp, protruding from his narrow face. The one arm was helpless in its sling, but he waved the other one. "Beneath this bandage, the blisters. But I cannot remove . . ."

"Take off the bandage."

"Please, El Gallo . . ."

"The bandage!" he roared.

Santos stood still, face hollow from terror, skinny legs shaking inside the fancy trousers he'd taken from the dead body of the army officer. Then he obeyed, pulling off the dirty bandages with his teeth. His hand bore a bullet wound, but not a burn.

"Hah!" El Gallo stepped back. Only his hat and his shoulders were visible over the roof. Santos screamed and turned, starting to run. Loose stones rolled beneath his boots. He fell, catching himself on an outflung hand. A gun smashed the air. The report was flat, muffled by heat. The bullet struck Santos in the breast, turning him over. He ended on his face with only enough left for an agonized clutch of his hand. El Gallo was hunched with powder smoke drifting past his face.

He grunted something, and his right shoulder moved in re-holstering the gun. Then he turned and walked from sight. Scarcely a minute later Garrett could hear him snoring inside the hut. He was having a *siesta*.

Garrett had seen a good many dead men during

73

his years along the border, but the brutality of this particular execution left him a little bit sick. He wished he had a smoke, and decided to risk taking one. He rolled one, lighted it. He had an idea. El Gallo came to meet someone other than Santos.

*You have failed,* El Gallo had said, *and your failing has made El Gallo the great fool.* He'd been referring to that ambush in Cañon Puerta, so there must have been some connection between El Gallo and Millerick, owner of the Block M. He had nothing to do but think about those things as he hunkered there, hot and thirsty, smoking the cigarette.

A rider came in sight, following the crooked arroyo bottom from the direction of the Río Grande. *Gringo,* by his appearance, his horse a high-blooded bay. Millerick. Garrett wasn't surprised.

He crouched forward a trifle, for the mesquite gave only partial concealment, but Millerick had caught sight of Santos's body, lying in the sun, and his eyes remained on him through all of his last 100 yards.

The *clatter* of hoofs aroused El Gallo who came in sight with eyes narrowed against sun glare after his short sleep.

"What the devil?" Millerick asked in his womanish voice. He tried to give the voice command and authority, and succeeded only in imparting a screechy edge. He jerked his head at Santos. "What's that?"

"Thees?" El Gallo spat in the direction of Santos's body. "Sometimes is foolish traitor careless when he clean gun."

"You killed him."

"El Gallo kill? Ha! Ha-ha! Ho-ho ha!" His laughter came in successive bursts, each lower than the last. Then the laugh ended, leaving nothing but a grimace on his whip-swollen lips. "Thees man traitor. So. Yesterday he work for El Gallo. *Mañana*, perhaps, for someone else's gold. So El Gallo use each traitor but once, like cigarette."

Millerick swung down from his horse. His eyes kept shifting over, resting on Santos's body. Perspiration had appeared on his upper lip, and he wiped it away. There were two ivory-handled Colt revolvers on his hips, and, as though by accident, he kept his right hand hooked just over one butt.

"It's your business, Gallo," he said in his treble.

El Gallo had a swig from the canteen. "Drink?"

"Sure."

Millerick took the canteen, drank, using one hand. El Gallo noticed and his heavy lips twisted in a smile, but he said nothing.

Millerick handed the canteen back and stood for a moment, a powerful and erect figure, thinking things over. He was a handsome man, utterly unlike his unfortunate voice. He was the type that anyone, man or woman, would call handsome—

up to the time he moved or said something. His voice and swagger spoiled everything. He was too sure, too domineering. Garrett had thought some about the man and had come to the conclusion it was his voice that was at the bottom of it. He was self-conscious about it, and his overbearing manner was an attempt to compensate. But he was handsome, swagger or not. Thirty-five or thirty-eight years old, 190 pounds of smooth muscle.

Millerick walked out of sight, dropped his voice, and said something.

El Gallo cried back: "Not gold, but guns, *Señor* Gringo."

Millerick's answer was too low. Garrett wanted to hear the conversation, especially Millerick's end of it. He moved down a trifle, finding his way through twisted mesquite trunks, avoiding loose dirt and stones. A rattlesnake had been coiled, sleeping in the sun. Garrett saw the reptile and tried to move back, to prevent the sharp movement that would disturb it. No chance on that steep slope. He slid a little, dropped to hands, catching himself, drew back his boot. The rattles sounded, their noise loud as beans rattled in a dry gourd. The snake lashed out, barely missing Garrett's boot, and retreated, coiling again, leaving venom on the rocks.

Millerick cried—"Rattler!"—and sprang away from the shack. Garrett whipped the .44 from its holster, aimed, pulled the trigger all in one practiced movement. The bullet struck, cutting half through the snake's scaly neck, left him writhing, sliding down the slope.

"Millerick!" Garrett cried. He lowered the gun, but still kept it in his hand. "It's only me, killing a snake. You don't need to draw." He said it pleasantly, but it was a warning just the same, and Millerick took it, got his hand clear of the ivory gun butt, backed into the open. El Gallo stood out of sight. Garrett went on in an ordinary tone: "I wouldn't have come sneaking up if I'd known it was you, but I heard a shot and I've been imagining *bandidos* behind every bush."

He slid down the bank, gun still ready. El Gallo was standing in front of the shack with a pistol in each hand.

"Put 'em away, *caballero*," Garrett drawled.

El Gallo leaned forward, mouth twisted down at the corners, face ugly and swollen.

"Put them away!"

"*Sí.*"

He slid the guns back with a truculent movement. His little pig eyes were on Garrett's face. It had been dark at the *cantina*, but there was still a good chance Gallo would recognize him. He didn't particularly give a damn, but it would be better to make Millerick think he suspected nothing.

He jerked his head at Santos's body: "Trouble?"

Millerick answered, making his squeaky treble

loud in an attempt to give it substance. "You don't need to look at me, Garrett. I got here just a second ago myself." He nodded to El Gallo. "If this *caballero* chooses that way to settle disputes . . ." He shrugged.

"Why sure," drawled Garrett. "Just so it ain't us. What the hell?"

His answer pleased Millerick. The man evidently did not suspect Garrett had been hiding close above the shack when he rode up. Millerick expected his lie to be believed.

El Gallo was looking intently at Garrett's face. "I have seen you some place before, *señor*."

"I been around a little." Then to Millerick, indicating El Gallo: "Who's your friend?"

"Friend? He's no friend of mine. He was here, waiting for me." He turned and faced El Gallo. "Well, what was it you wanted?"

"Notheeng, *señor*. I only wait here through *siesta*."

"*Siesta*'s over. Your horse is saddled. Get moving."

"As you say," he growled.

El Gallo got his canteen, his serape, and walked inside the corral, dragging big-rowelled spurs in the dust. He swung to the saddle and drove spurs, spinning the mustang along. At that moment he remembered Santos's mustang, and took the bridle.

"Sure! As you say . . . as *grande señor* say . . . thees poor *caballero* will do!"

# VII

They watched him ride away, and, when he was gone, Millerick made a pretense of relief by shaking out a handkerchief and wiping his forehead.

"Damn! You were a welcome sight. I spent a bad minute or two when I rode up and found him waiting here. A *bandido* if I ever saw one."

"El Gallo."

"That was El Gallo?" He opened his eyes wide, showing surprise.

"Sure. And it's open season on *gringo* ranchers this side of the border. You were lucky." Then he changed the subject. "How did you get along at the head end of that cañon last night?"

Millerick made a wry face. "You were right about them knowing the cañon. They just faded away. Up rock walls . . . everywhere."

"Think this Gallo had a hand in it?"

"Maybe. But there are a thousand *bandidos* along the border. It could have been any of them."

"Ever hear of The Angel?"

Millerick smiled and said in a musing treble: "The Angel . . . a masked woman who looks like an angel and rides like a devil. Yes, I've heard of her."

"I followed her last night to Río Jacinto."

"And lost her?"

"I haven't got her with me, have I?"

"There's an international boundary, of course. . . ."

"To hell with the international boundary."

Millerick jerked his head and laughed. "Say, I believe you really mean it."

"The boundary doesn't seem to mean much to you, either."

"I own ranches on both sides. Besides, the *caballería* is somewhat indebted to me. I'm going to see their officers now." He jerked his head toward the southeast. "To Gallegos."

Garrett watched Millerick remount and ride away along the arroyo. The route could take him to Gallegos, a *caballería* garrison on the Ojo Caliente, but Garrett had an idea he was lying just as he'd been lying about knowing El Gallo, but Garrett did not risk following him. Instead, he rode across the Río to the Block M home ranch where he ate supper and roped a fresh mustang from his own string. He went back then, swiftly, through the cool evening, not toward the arroyo, but cutting cross country toward Casa Grande, the old *residencia* of the Torretagles outfit. If Millerick was indeed headed for Gallegos, he would almost certainly pause at Casa Grande for the night.

The moon was an hour above the horizon when Garrett stopped on the rimrock with the *hacienda* lying below him. It was one of the great old-time spreads, this Casa Grande, headquarters of the historic Torretagles grant. It dated further back than an American could imagine—back to the days when the Pilgrim fathers were still fighting the Indians around Plymouth colony. A land grant from the King of Spain, it had once been larger than many countries of Europe, and had been ruled by the Torretagles, father and son, for a half dozen generations. But the Texas secession had cut it in half, and the squeeze of raiders from both sides of the border were weakening it until the empire was a mere shell of its former grandeur, ready to be divided among the new powers of the country—men like Millerick and El Gallo.

Still, looked at from a distance, by moonlight, it seemed to be great as ever. It lay in a broad valley, between cliffs and columns of quartzite. Springs rose in numerous places along some sandstone shelves, the water from them forming brooks that meandered across meadows and later joined to form the Bahía Pequeña that, in wet years, flowed all the way to the Río Grande.

With an unfailing supply of water for irrigation there were cornfields, gardens, and orchards. There was a village of peon huts, each with its tiny square of garden, then many acres of sheds, corrals, and bunkhouses, and finally the great *residencia* itself, a white adobe building of many wings and patios.

Light shone in the big salon of the *residencia*.

Perhaps *Señorita* Camila Torretagles, last survivor of the direct line, was entertaining guests.

Garrett rode down the trail, followed a roadway of crushed stone laid by peons a century before, and now turned hard as pavement. The roadway was ditched on both sides, and extended straight as a rifle shot across creek, meadow, and garden. No one challenged him. He turned off a quarter mile short of the house and followed a side road among corrals.

Now, at closer view, he could see Casa Grande for what it really was. The corrals that looked so well planned from above were falling apart from lack of repair, their earth untrodden and springing up to grass and weeds. Barns were without roofs, and house after house that had once been home to *vaquero* and overseer were empty and dark. A cluster of corrals, barns, and bunkhouses were still in use. There was a large corral, higher than most, with about twenty horses inside it. He peered through the rails. Mustangs. In a second, smaller corral, he caught sight of Millerick's bay.

He'd been wrong, then, in supposing the man was headed for the Río Jacinto. Perhaps he actually was going to Gallegos as he had said.

Someone was plucking a guitar, tenor voice raised in the fluid notes of a Spanish love song. Garrett followed the sound and came across ten or twelve men in *vaquero* trappings seated beneath the shadow of a pole awning before a bunkhouse, their positions marked by the coals of their strong Mexican cigarettes.

The guitar stopped abruptly and there were seconds of silence as they watched his approach.

"¡*Vaqueros*!" he said as he dismounted, and they instantly knew by the inflection of his voice that he was a *gringo*. He went on, speaking in Spanish, saying that he'd ridden over from Texas, looking for a friend. Could any of them tell him where he could find Millerick, owner of the bay horse?

Finally a heavy, clownish-faced man spoke: "The bay horse, he is perhaps mine, *señor*."

He was lying, of course. Garrett shrugged, stood with one shoulder against the awning post, twisting up a cigarette. He put it between his lips, struck a match. Light of the match struck strongly across the lean lines of his face. He flipped the match away. All the while he'd watched the clownish-faced *vaquero* who had moved to the door of the bunkhouse and was standing, blocking his way as though he expected Garrett to push his way inside.

Garrett walked forward, and his superior height allowed him to look across the man's shoulder.

A grease-dip burned inside showing a skinny old Mexican lying in a bunk, his chest bound around with bandage. Garrett recognized him. He'd glimpsed his face at Cañon Puerta the night before—the man who had ridden away, wounded, held in the saddle by means of a belt hooked over the saddle horn.

The clownish-faced one lunged forward to thrust him away, but the movement had come too late.

"Why did you peep inside, *gringo*?"

Garrett stepped back, laughing. "What is this . . . Casa Grande de Torretagles, or some den on the Río Jacinto?"

The man started to answer, stopped.

Garrett realized there was someone behind him. He spun, hand instinctively falling to his gun.

"No, *señor*." It was a heavy voice, unfamiliar. "Do not reach for your gun. What do you do here?"

The man was massive, old, and he supported himself on a diamond willow crutch. He had a broad, sun-blackened face with hair and moustache white as cotton. There was a pistol at his waist— a long-barreled one identical to the gun The Angel had carried. The swivel holster was identical, too.

The man went on: "Men call me Juan. I am for many years *caporal* here. As you say . . . foreman."

"Smith. John Smith."

"Of course. All Americans are named Smith. You saw the wounded man inside? There are many ways men become wounded, no? And it is our way here, at Casa Grande, to give the wounded care and shelter with no questions asked."

"And I haven't asked any."

Juan nodded. "So. You are welcome." The clownish one started to object, but Juan cut him off. "Yes, Paraso, he is welcome."

Juan clapped his hands, calling a young peon who went to care for Garrett's mustang.

"You are hungry, Americano Smith? I think perhaps the *cocinero* has left the beef and beans."

"Thanks," Garrett said.

He'd eaten at the Block M, but the ride had left him hungry, and it was an opportunity to get away by himself. He ate a little inside the long, adobe mess house. When he stepped back outside, there was a movement in shadow beside the door. He turned, and was rammed by the hard muzzle of a Colt revolver.

"Hello, Ranger!"

It was an American voice. Familiar. From far back. Garrett couldn't remember where. The man moved so moonlight revealed his face. He knew then. It was Alvin Tucker, that coach robber from north of Pecos.

"Why, hello, Tucker."

Tucker grinned with a twist of his hard-slashed mouth. "I thought you'd remember me, Garrett. You Texas Rangers are all the same. All you ever forget are the faces of dead men."

Garrett laughed with a soft sound like the musical drawl of his voice. "Think I came down here looking for you?"

"No. I ain't that big a damn' fool. As long as I stay this side of the Río, you don't give a hoot." He still held the gun, not cocked, just with his thumb hooked over the hammer. "You're the one who set the deadfall in Cañon Puerto last night, weren't you?"

"If I'd set it, you wouldn't even be here."

Tucker laughed. "But when it misfired, you were the one with brains to trail us. You're not like Millerick. He swaggers and beats his chest, and you just sit with your mouth shut. But all the same, you're the one that knows what goes on."

"Maybe Millerick knows, too. Ever think of that?"

"I've thought of it, but damned if he'd walk in at Casa Grande and show his back to three of the gang at the bunkhouse if he knew about it. Not Millerick. He's got guts, but he plays things safe just the same."

"He's at the house, isn't he?"

"You know damned well he is."

"Why did Paraso lie to me?"

"Spanish pride, m'boy. Millerick took over the Block M, the ranch that used to be the Torretagles' Casa del Norte. And he'll take over here when he wants, but these faithful old boys won't even admit he exists. Honor of the name. You never think of greasers having feelings like white men, but I guess all humans are pretty much the same."

"Who else is up there?"

"I never go near the *residencia*. If I did, old Juan would chuck me off the ranch." He jiggled the gun muzzle. "All right, Ranger, open up. What you doing here?"

"I told you. I'm following Millerick."

"To tell him about me, and poor Esteban?"

"No. I dare say Millerick already knows a hell of a lot more than you think he does."

"*No sabe.*"

"All right, how does El Gallo fit into the picture? Who paid over the gold to Santos and Miguel? Why did Santos kill Miguel and El Gallo kill Santos? What did they know that El Gallo didn't want told? Why did Millerick meet El Gallo in an arroyo this afternoon? And who is The Angel . . . or the Hija de Satanás . . . as the peons call her? Do you know those answers, Tucker? Neither do I. And that's why I'm here. I don't give a particular damn about you and your bug-crawling *bandidos*. The hell with you. I'm after big game."

"Big as El Gallo?"

"If he was all I wanted, I'd have killed him last night. And if you're still thinking about yourself, forget it. You're dead, and you'll stay dead long as you're on this side of the line. But don't come back, or you'll end up on the end of a reata cravat. Now stop acting like a damned fool and put up the gun."

Tucker heard him with an off-center smile

twisting his thin, predatory face. "Well, by damn! I never thought I'd be talked into anything by a Ranger." He slid the gun back in its holster.

"I'll keep my promise," Garrett said softly. "Just like I always have."

"Sure you will. And that about the reata cravat, too. I'll lay dollars to *pesos* you'd tie the knot yourself."

"No. I think I'd bury you right where I had to shoot you. You're not the kind that comes in alive." Then he asked: "Who's The Angel?"

"*¿Quién sabe?*"

"You mean you ride with her and don't know who she is?"

"That's what I mean."

"But Juan, that crippled old foreman, he knows!"

"You *are* sharp, aren't you. Damned sharp. Well, listen, don't let old Juan catch you snooping this lay because he's just the boy that will blast you with his Forty-Four."

Garrett left him there, climbed a rail fence, and walked through stunted pecan trees to the *residencia*.

The place was bigger, more sprawling, and older than it had seemed from above. Whole wings of it had been closed off and abandoned. There was light coming from a kitchen door and he circled it, keeping in shadow, and reached a patio shaded by wooden awnings and orange trees. Water was carried across the patio by a masonry gutter, and it made little, gurgling sounds in the dark.

He could see inside a big room. A dozen candles burned in the holders of an ornate silver candelabra, casting light on a table of polished Honduras mahogany, and to the mosaic tiles of a floor that stretched away toward the room's shadowy limits. No movement. No sign of anyone.

He kept going, circling the patio, passing beneath arches and pillars in imitation of the Moorish colonnades of old Spain. Shadow deep beneath it. He walked carefully, watching each step to keep his boots from sounding on loose flagstones.

A woman's voice sounded—unexpectedly close. He thought for a second she'd spoken to him. A soft, Spanish voice. Recognition struck him. It was different, and yet something about it was the same. Unmistakable. The woman of the night before—the masked woman of the *cantina*. He stood still, shoulder touching the adobe wall, deep shadow covering him.

She was talking. "There are many reasons a girl of my race would not marry an American, *Señor* Millerick."

Millerick's voice cut in. "Girl, I've told you enough times not to call me *Señor* Millerick. Do you know how it makes me feel when you call me that? I'll tell you. I feel like a usurer in a black silk hat come to foreclose the mortgage." He spoke slowly, trying to give substance to his womanish voice, to give it a mellow easiness.

She laughed a little: "Eh so, *señor*?"

"Please call me Ross."

He had an oily personality, and he was putting it on for the girl. Sound of his voice made Garrett detest him more than ever. He moved on a little, trying to get a glimpse of them.

He saw her then. She was dressed in a lacy gown of Spanish silk with its breast cut low. Moonlight and candle glow mixed, bringing out the soft curves of her shoulders. A black mantilla was over her head. He'd seen many women in mantillas, but all of them had had black, glossy hair. This girl was brunette. He'd always heard there were English women among the wives of the Torretagles. The mantilla did something unexpected to her coils of hair, gave her an extra measure of femininity. She seemed much younger than the girl of the *cantina*. She was twenty, perhaps. Only her voice seemed the same, and now, after seeing her, he couldn't be sure of that.

"Ross." She repeated the name as though getting her tongue used to it. "Ross."

"And I'm no banker in a high silk hat."

"Of course. But one must pay debts. You will take the thousand *pesos*, *señor*."

The *pesos* were in gold dubloons and she had stacked them in a small pillar on a table.

"Listen, girl . . ."

"You will take them, *señor*. According to the agreement of my father. God willing, you will receive more from these Torretagles fingers. At the rate of a thousand *pesos* each month until the grant can be delivered me."

Millerick was standing, legs wide and hands on hips, looking at the money. His back was toward Garrett, but he could guess the expression on his face. Finally he lifted his broad shoulders in a shrug of unwilling helplessness and raked the money over the table edge, dropping it in his pocket. The gold coins weighted his coat like a lump of bullet lead.

"Very well, Camila."

"You will call me *Señorita* Torretagles," she said pleasantly enough. "Now the receipt, if you please."

There was a quill pen and well of ink handy. He scratched a few words, and she folded the paper, slipped it inside her bodice. Millerick stood looking down at her.

"Why do you build such a fortress around yourself? You know how I care for you."

"Indeed."

"Yes. And I'm vain enough to think you care for me, if you'd be truthful with yourself. This ranch has become an obsession with you. Holding it together, bringing it back to its former glory. Well, I'll tell you this, *Señorita* Camila, the old days are gone in Mexico since that Indian, Juárez, came to power with his so-called Republic. He wants nothing but to chop up the great estates and divide the land among peons. There is only one way to make Casa Grande great once more, and that is by business methods. Yes, *gringo* business methods. Not with lazy peons and a half million cattle wild as antelope with spines that resemble razor-back hogs, but with blooded stock, the new stock they're developing in America, the stock I'm bringing to the Block M. Think of what *we* could do with Casa Grande . . . you and I. We could raise such cattle here for next to nothing, then drive north to the fat prairies of Kansas, and beyond to the Platte and Yellowstone."

She said softly: "But Casa Grande would be Casa Grande no longer. It would be Block M, an American ranch."

"Call it what you like. Call it Casa Grande. Torretagles. I'd even change my name. Such things mean nothing to me." He had brought himself to a fine stage of oratory, but his womanish voice spoiled its entire effect. "Think it over, *señorita*. Think of that when you give your answer."

"You're asking me to marry you?"

"For the tenth time, I am asking you to be my wife. You've always put me off, remember? Tonight I came for a final answer. A yes or no."

"No."

The word was soft as a cat's paw, but it struck

him hard. He started to turn, checked himself, and took a stride toward her. She stood her ground, straight, slim-waisted, looking girlish in the lacy gown.

He said: "You talk about Casa Grande being your trust. About you, the last of the great Torretagles, saving it, and yet you turn away the one man who could save it for you."

She laughed, and suddenly her voice had the whip-like taunt he'd heard in the *cantina* last night: "Who now comes like black hat banker with mortgage, *señor*?"

She stood, toes of her slippers barely showing beneath the filmy cascades of her dress, bare arms at her sides, lips thin and smiling a little. Millerick stood close in front of her, and she looked tiny by comparison.

"No!" he said. "I'm not a banker. I'm a man, and you're a beautiful woman."

His hands reached, closed, fingers sinking deep in the bare flesh of her shoulders. Although she knew his temper, she'd evidently had no idea he'd actually lay hands on her. She twisted from side to side, trying to free herself.

"Let me go!" she hissed.

"No, girl. You can't play cat with me any longer."

She was unexpectedly strong. Her hands found his wrists, tore herself free. But he seized her again, arms closing around her back.

"I will call Juan! Juan would kill . . . !"

"You will not call Juan, for if he killed me, my Eastern backers would take over Casa Grande within a month, and then what would there be for you, an aristocrat without money, but a nunnery or some rich old man of Cuidad Méjico?"

"Let me go!"

He laughed and drew her close. For a second her face was close to his. Garrett was walking across the flagstones of the patio, but neither of them knew. He spoke, and the voice so close made Millerick release her and whirl around.

For a second he was crouched forward, peering at Garrett's face. "You, Ranger!"

"Yes."

"Damn you. You followed me. What business do you have snooping in my affairs? I could have you . . ."

"You called me in to help with your affairs, remember?"

Millerick turned in a movement that swung the ivory gun butt away from his right hip. His hand went down swiftly, but Garrett knew it was coming. His fist lashed in a sudden arc, connecting flushly with Millerick's jaw. His head snapped back. He reeled. One boot heel caught a flagstone. He went down, catching himself on backflung elbows. Eyes rolled off focus. The gun was still half holstered. He reached for it again. Garrett kicked and sent it bounding across the flagstones.

Millerick lunged forward, wrapping arms around Garrett's legs. Garrett twisted back, trying to boot his way free. The man was too powerful, hanging on, rising while charging forward. Garrett was hurled, back and shoulders to the patio floor.

Garrett doubled legs as he fell. They uncoiled, smashing Millerick in the abdomen. Millerick rolled back, caught himself. His left hand was reaching for the second pistol.

"No!" It was the voice of the girl. "I have a gun, *Señor* Millerick. It is cocked and aimed at your heart. I do not wish to pull the trigger."

Millerick stopped, stood for a moment facing Garrett, chest rising and falling with deep breathing. His dark, pomaded hair had fallen across his face and he fingered it out of the way.

"All right," he said in his womanish treble. "All right, *señorita*. "But you understand . . ."

"I understand you have in you pocket one thousand *pesos*, and that a month from now you will get another thousand, and the month after that a thousand more until the land grant which you had stolen from the archives in Chihuahua City is once more the property of Torretagles."

"*Señorita* . . ."

"Get out."

"You heard the lady," Garrett drawled. "Get out."

Millerick still fingered his pomaded hair, his handsome face savage from frustration. He hissed a vile word through clenched teeth, turned, located his sombrero, put it on. Someone had stepped on it, treading it out of shape. The girl released the hammer to safety, tossed the gun to him; he caught it by the barrel, re-holstered it, then without saying another word spun and strode away, disappearing among the shadows of the pecan trees.

For the first time then Camila Torretagles really looked at Garrett. There was no sign of recognition in her eyes, no apparent memory of him from the *cantina*. She seemed much smaller in slippers than she had in riding boots. Small and feminine and young. He noticed that Millerick's fingers had left red bruises on the soft, white flesh of her shoulders.

"Who are you?" she asked quietly.

He didn't answer right away. Suddenly, after the raw violence, everything had changed. He noticed how cool the night was, smelled the perfume of growing things, heard the liquid music of water running across the patio in its masonry gutter. The night had a dream-like quality he did not want to disturb. But she had asked him a question. He answered: "I'm a Texas Ranger. Like he said. Tom Garrett."

"A Texas Ranger in Méjico?"

"I go lots of places where I'm not invited." He paused and added: "I even go to the *cantina de Pablo Alvarez* in Lagunas."

He was watching her face, but no shadow of

surprise crossed it. She thought for a moment and shrugged with one white shoulder. "Then you are so brave?"

"Not brave, just curious. I followed a masked woman there last night."

"Indeed. Then it must have been the Hija de Satanás. You have heard of her?"

"Yes, I've heard of her."

"But why do you tell me, *Señor* Ranger?"

"Because a couple of times tonight I heard her voice."

"Her voice?" She smiled a very little. Her hand reached, and, as if by accident, her long, aristocratic fingers touched the front of his shirt. "I think you are mistaken. There is no daughter of Satan here. But what if there were? What would you, a Texas Ranger Americano . . . ?"

"I'm not sure what I would do."

"Perhaps you would fight at her side, like you fought at my side tonight."

"That depends."

"On what, *señor*?"

"On whether I was here in Chihuahua, or across the Río in Texas. I'm not a Ranger over here."

"I see." She was smiling up at him, fingers playing with a loose button on the front of his shirt. "If I ever see that Hija de Satanás, I will tell her to shoot you only in Texas."

The way she put it struck him as being funny. He laughed.

She said: "But what if she raids in Texas only to take what is rightly hers?"

"Then she'd better tell me all about it?"

"Some men are willing to ride beside her with only her word that it is so."

"I'm a Ranger, not a coach robber like Tucker."

"Ah, so."

"Or a brigand like El Gallo. Don't take it as an unfailing rule, but generally you can go further on a Ranger's word than you can on the word of a coach robber or a brigand."

"Tucker? It is he you're . . . ?"

"No. I've known Tucker for a long time, and I think it's too bad he got to riding up the wrong side of the trail. I'm talking about El Gallo. I think if The Angel compared the doubloons from Miguel's purse and the doubloons from El Gallo's, she'd find they were pretty much the same. She might even find out they all came from Millerick in the first place."

"If I ever see her, I will tell her."

"And if she ever rides north of the Río again, it would be best not to let El Gallo know her plans."

"And that, too, *señor*." She was looking down at his wrist, the one that had been bitten when The Angel escaped the night before. "Your wrist! Something bit it?"

He grinned. "A wildcat."

"Ah, so! You must let me put on some hot fat

pork to draw out the poison. Such wounds can be dangerous. I want you to live so that someday you may meet that Angel again."

"Why sure," he said in his easy drawl. "But I'd rather meet *Señorita* Camila Torretagles. A whole lot I'd rather."

# VIII

There had been a haze from distant winds in the sky all day, and toward evening bullet-gray clouds commenced piling up along the horizon. It was getting on toward early twilight when fourteen riders came down from the deep cut of Río Jacinto, dismounted, and waited in brush cover on the Mexico side of the Río Grande.

They talked little, mostly in monosyllables, and either hunkered with hand-rolled cigarettes between their lips or spent their time inspecting guns, or adjusting latigo straps. Their leader, a slim, arrogant-appearing girl in black sombrero and black mask, rode back on her stallion after reconnoitering the riverbank, and gave a signal that started the men swinging to their saddles. The girl was the *bandido* leader known as The Angel.

She kept them there on nervous mustangs for a last few moments of inspection. At least half of the men had not been on her previous raid across the Río, but some of the faces were familiar. There was the clownish-faced Paraso, Esteban holding himself stiffly because of bandages, Tucker with the inevitable dead cigarette in his hard-slashed mouth, little Chico, the Apache renegade riding with a blanket instead of a saddle.

"Any questions?" she asked. Then, when no one answered, she said to Paraso: "Tell me what you are to do?"

"While you drive cattle home from *rancho*, Chico and I will make trouble at the Poniente fields where perhaps waits ambush. Ha! How would your Paraso forget so simple a thing?"

"Very well, but be sure they follow you. That's why you and Chico have the fastest horses. Let them follow you. But don't be too brave. I would not have you killed. Lead them away, and lose them at Morella Crossing. From there you will circle back and meet us in the caves near El Gallo's camp up Jacinto. *¿Sabe?*"

Paraso and Chico both nodded.

She turned to the others. "For us it will be the Block M home ranch. There should be seven or eight hundred cattle waiting, and we can get them to Jacinto by dawn."

Tucker said: "And then to visit El Gallo."

"Not El Gallo. The swine will not be there. I doubt there will be more than five of his snakes, and them drunk as usual. Our only trouble will be finding his cache of gold when we shoot them."

The Apache spoke: "Give me one. Alive. Me

100

know . . . trick. Apache trick. For make talk. Me know . . ."

"I'll bet you do!" Tucker said with his wry mouth.

*"Ha-ah-ah-ah!"* cried the Apache, jerking back his bronze colored face. It wasn't often the Apache laughed, and this time it was not particularly good to see.

The Angel: "We will find the gold without torture, I think."

Her plan was swift and daring. The timing and boldness of it had captured the men's imaginations. The Angel had told El Gallo she planned to raid the Poniente fields of the Block M knowing he would carry the information to Millerick. Paraso and Chico would be sent as a diversion, stir the expected ambush, and lead Millerick's men to the east. At the same instant, with the home ranch left unguarded or nearly so, she would take possession, drive off the cattle already brought in on the beef roundup, and hold them in one of the blind cañons of the Río Jacinto. But her plan did not end there, for once more she had arranged a rendezvous with El Gallo at the *cantina* in Lagunas, a rendezvous she did not intend to keep. She had located El Gallo's headquarters retreat deep in the Jacinto country, and, while the *bandido* chief waited for her in Lagunas, she would raid it.

The Angel had one last look at her men, then she

signaled with her coiled *cuerda* and splashed down through mud and water to cross the Río.

Darkness had a muggy quality. There were slight currents of wind, sometimes from one direction and sometimes another. No sunset. The clouds had deeply covered it. There would be no moon, but light always hung to those mesas and prairies even on the darkest nights, so they'd see well enough to drive the cattle to Jacinto.

She reached the other side, only this time she did not follow the deep arroyo, but turned boldly up the main road that connected the Block M with Casa Grande.

"We should have come by daylight," Tucker muttered, easing his mustang up beside her.

"So, American, you call me too bold."

"You're the boss, lady."

"So I am bold." She laughed, emphasizing the sound with a *jingle* of the silver ornaments on her sombrero. "Millerick knows I would not be such a fool as to take this trail. And so we are here."

"Ever hear of a man named Garrett?"

She turned and peered at his face through the dark. "The Ranger?"

"Sure. The Ranger. He might act different on this side of the border."

"What do you know about . . . ?" She stopped, and obviously altered what she had started to say. "About him?"

Tucker laughed. "I don't know a damned thing. I'm just a good guesser."

"So what would you guess?"

"I'd guess he had more figured out than you think. We might just run into him out there in the dark."

She thought for a while, and spoke: "We will not meet him. Or anyone. Only the flunky, the *cocinero*, perhaps some *gringo* coward guest such as the great man with the squeaky voice likes to bring from Abilene."

"Maybe. Maybe you have him tricked. He's not so old, that Ranger, but he's lone-wolfed it, and he's lost some toes in the trap, so don't get the idea he fools easy."

It was a two-hour ride to the Block M. The night was darker than ever. Occasional flashes of lightning cut the sky, bringing the country into view. Wind, and then a few big spatters of rain.

"We stampede them steer sure tonight!" Esteban hissed, more to himself than anyone. He always talked to himself, under his breath, and tonight he kept hitching himself to one side, bothered by that half-healed bullet wound.

The road took them to Sarita Valley, across some grassy bottoms, miles in extent, lying between mesa rims. A streambed meandered here and there, and, although it had been weeks since the last rain, there was water, seeped through gravel from above, lying clear and warm in tiny potholes.

She left the road unexpectedly and cut across some dry lakebeds, rough from hoof marks pressed there the spring before, swung close to the heaped talus rock at the face of a mesa, and from that vantage point looked at the country away and below.

After a time, two pinpoints of light became visible—candles burning in the big house. It was about two miles away.

She sat for a while, but it was impossible to tell anything for certain. No light in the bunkhouse, but the crew might be there for all that. She signaled and rode down across gently sloping fields.

Willows and cottonwoods grew in clumps along a creek. The riders moved across a wide ford where water scarcely covered a horse's hoof. There were the usual ranch odors of hay, and corrals, and blacksmith shop.

"I will go on alone." The Angel swung her stallion across the trail, blocking the way.

Esteban started to remonstrate, but she quieted him with an impatient gesture of her *cuerda*. "Wait here. I'll be back in ten minutes."

She let the stallion move on up the bank and around the brushy edge of a meadow. She drew up suddenly and turned in the saddle, thinking one of her men had followed her. Then she knew. It was Tom Garrett. Tucker had been right.

Her hand instinctively dropped to the Colt in its swing holster.

"No, *Señorita* Angel," he said.

He had his gun drawn, barrel angled toward the sky, his thumb crooked over the hammer.

She looked at it and laughed. "Do you shoot women in Texas?"

"I never had to yet. And I don't reckon I'll have to tonight. I've been waitin' for you."

"You knew I'd come?"

"Why, yes. Tonight, or tomorrow, or the night after. I knew you'd come before Millerick started moving his beef cut north." He was smiling in his old, easy way. "But I didn't expect you to make the raid all alone. Where are your boys?"

She had no intention of answering, and the twist of her lips showed it. "Well, what do you do? Arrest me, perhaps? Take me to your *gringo* jail? Make yourself the hero . . . you, *Señor* Garrett, the Texas Ranger who captured The Angel?"

"I'm takin' you to no jail. I been waitin' out here to do you a favor. I wanted to tell you that another raid would just be playing Millerick's game. I've done a little snooping the past couple of weeks. You think he's turned up a land grant that takes precedence over the old Torretagles papers in the Chihuahua archives. Hell, it was a forgery, and he got testimony by bribing those crooked officials. He'd never made it stand if old Ramón had lived. Ramón wouldn't have given him five *centavos*. The paper would never stand up in a court not riddled with graft. He's using it for a squeeze on Casa Grande to make the beautiful *Señorita* Camila get herself in more trouble than a regiment of Rangers could get her out of. Don't you under-stand that . . . he *wants* you to pull this raid across the line?"

She sat straight with her head high, looking at him. Then the corners of her mouth twisted down and she said: "Of course! You and the American game. You, the Ranger! I've heard how clever you men of the Texas Rangers were. You are one against many, and know this is the only way to stop us. By making us believe . . ."

"I could stop you all right, but there's no use of letting you get killed."

"It would be fine. You, the lone hand, to turn back fourteen of the hardest-riding *bandidos* on the border. Then you could laugh at *Señor* Millerick, couldn't you? You could say . . . 'You, with your ambush, catch no one, while I, single-handed, send them all running across the border without firing a shot.' "

"You don't believe that."

She laughed with a tone that showed she did believe it.

He said: "Millerick is several things, but one of them isn't a fool. He knew there was a reason for El Gallo killing Santos and decided it was because Santos had talked too much to you. Therefore, seeing you knew what El Gallo's game was, Millerick was certain any information you gave the *bandido* was false. I don't know what you're planning tonight but there's a good chance you haven't got Millerick fooled. He'll be ready for you."

"Where is his ambush, Ranger?"

"I don't know where it is or whether he has one. Do you think Millerick would tell me anything after that battle we had back at Casa Grande? I don't know what his plans are."

"He is ambushed at the Poniente."

"All right, maybe he is. And maybe not. But I'll bet dollars to *pesos* you'll go back across the Río with plenty of empty saddles if you try this raid tonight."

She laughed with a derisive toss of her head. "But we will raid, *señor*. We are not to be stopped by one Ranger."

He brought the gun down a trifle. "Yes, you are. You're stopping right here."

The girl scarcely looked at the pistol. She was peering at the darkness behind him. Her lips were smiling a little. "You would then kill me?"

"I'll do what I have to. I can shoot the horse from under you. If you go for your gun, I can shoot it from your hand like you did Santos."

"You talk of shooting me and all the while my Esteban is back of you with a pistol aimed at your brain."

Garrett did not look around. He sat as he had before, the gun almost leveled.

"You do not believe me?" she asked with a laugh in her voice.

"Expect me to? It's an old trick."

Wind was blowing, hissing through grass and willow branches hiding the approach of Esteban's horse, but the *click* of his gun being cocked cut the night and made Garret flinch. He sat rigidly, listening to the crunch of grass under hoofs, the *squeak* of saddle leather.

"And now, *señor*?" she said.

"Why, I reckon you got the ace," he drawled.

A man's voice behind him: "Drop the peestol!"

"Sure." Garrett's fingers opened, and his gun *thudded* to earth.

"Keep your hands clear," Esteban warned, leaning to pick up the gun.

"Don't worry. I ain't suicidal."

The Angel nudged her horse up beside him, took his Winchester from its saddle scabbard, saw the extra revolver, and plucked that, too. Darkness had covered her face until then, and now he could see her black mask, the smooth lines of her face beneath it, the few stray locks of brown-colored hair escaping her black sombrero. There was a wind-blown fragrance about her that made him remember that night on the patio at Casa Grande.

Esteban spoke: "Perhaps you should not watch while I keel him, *señorita*. It is not good that . . ."

"No, you will not kill. Perhaps he tells me true

108

about Millerick. Perhaps he lies. Let us wait and see."

"Ah, so," Esteban grumbled.

"You will ride with him to Río Jacinto."

"I, *señorita*? You mean that I, Esteban, go weeth him? That I, Esteban, your first horseman, ride away when we are too few already, just so this *gringo* . . . ?"

"You are wounded, Esteban. It is the best way."

Esteban faced her for a second, a skinny old man with rebellious eyes, then he jerked his shoulders in a sign of resignation. "Eh, so! As you say. But it would be so simple to keel him. Then, if he is a liar, we would not have this trouble for nothing."

"And if he told us true?"

"Why, then, I would say prayers for him in church." Esteban motioned with his gun. "Go, *Señor* Ranger. And do not tempt my gun. I have the jumpy trigger finger."

The girl watched them out of sight. A tightness showed in the lines of her mouth. She rode slowly, picking her way by memory around outlying sheds and corrals. Here and there a new fence of adobe building had been put up since Millerick took over the ranch but most of the ground she could have covered blindfolded.

Candlelight burned in the cook house where the *cocinero* was bent over a wooden tub, punching his arms elbow deep in bread dough. She drew up and watched him for a while. Over by the bunkhouse someone was playing a mouth organ, its reedy sound coming intermittently as the wind died and rose again. Some *gringo* tune.

Cowboys were gathered there. She went close enough to see the glow of their cigarettes. It surprised her to find so many left at the ranch, then she realized that there was a distinction between working cowboys and gunmen on a ranch run as a "business." The gunmen would be with Millerick if he'd laid that ambush at the Poniente fields.

She rode back to the cook house and the skinny old Mexican *cocinero*, hearing the *tinkle* of bit chains, pulled sticky hands from bread dough and peered out at her.

"Come outside!" she said.

The *cocinero* hesitated in the door, his eyes frightened as he made her out in the fringe of candlelight.

"The Angel," he whispered. "It is true . . . you are The Angel?"

"Yes."

"Do not kill me, *señorita*. Behold, I do not even carry the gun."

"Come outside. Walk ahead of me." She kept him moving at a trot until he was away from the buildings, then she stopped him and asked: "Is Millerick at the *residencia*?"

"Gone, *señorita*, gone . . . since maybe noon."

"The crew . . . are they all here?"

"Not all, *señorita*. But I am not sure. Me only poor *cocinero*."

She looked in his eyes. He was too frightened to lie. She gestured for him to keep going and took him on to the creek crossing. Men still waiting in the deep shadow. There were movements, a re-holstering of guns when they saw who she was.

"New recruit?" Tucker asked, looking at the *cocinero*, a laugh in his voice. Then he added: "Know that Esteban vamoosed?"

"I sent him back." She didn't bother to mention the Ranger. "Some cowboys are over by the bunkhouse. The *cocinero* says Millerick left about noon. We'll gamble on it."

They helped the old *cocinero* to mount, bareback, one of the two extra mustangs led by the *caballada* boy and headed through the willows and on a wide circle of the ranch buildings.

"*Nombre de Dios*," a *bandido* kept whispering. "What night for drive cattle."

The Apache renegade broke his silence of more than an hour by saying: "Maybe ambush. Dark night good for duck bullet."

They found cattle dotting some wide, grassy field west of the house, grass-fat steers, first installment of the beef roundup that would go north to Abilene on the big fall drive. No ambush here. Not enough cover on these flats. They turned the *cocinero* loose, knowing it would take him the better part of an hour to get back to the ranch and broke into two groups, swinging around the herd. It was well planned. Everything was as visualized. The Angel rode by herself, hunted the crest of a gentle knoll, and sat watching as her men commenced swinging *cuerdas* and rope goads, getting the cattle into motion.

Wind commenced, carrying rain. It increased and came in successive sheets, soaking through her *chaleco* and black silk shirt, running in streams from the brim of black sombrero, but she did not seem to notice.

Cattle were running, bellowing, but the sound of them was soaked up by the storm. They were headed as they should be, toward the south. Then a rider appeared unexpectedly, trying to turn them. At first she thought it was one of her own men, then she saw others, revealed by repeated lightning flashes. They were herders—Millerick's men. Night herders. Just awakened and not yet realizing that this was anything but a stampede of wild longhorns, frightened by thunder and storm. More men came in view, turning the lead steers, evidently trying to pocket them against some mesa faces which rose several miles to the west.

Gunfire cut the dark. Flashes of burning powder half a mile away. It was her *bandidos*. The bullets must have been close, for the night herders swung away from the herd and answered it.

She moved down from the knoll, keeping the

stallion at an easy lope. More of her men were riding past, their horses at a gallop through mud and rain. The Apache, two of the new recruits, Tucker, the *gringo*. Guns lashed out from the mouth of a dry wash and the Apache seemed to spin from his horse, but he was not hit. The renegade was holding mane with one hand, bent far over, using the side of his horse for protection as he went on at a dead run, and the next second he was firing from just over the horse's back.

More guns from the dry wash. All the Block M men seemed to have gathered there now. One of them had a Winchester and its high-pitched *whang* could be heard repeatedly over the heavy boom of Colt pistols.

The Angel drew up a quarter mile away and looked through stormy darkness toward the ranch wondering if gunfire would bring the rest of the crew. Probably not. Storm and wind would cover the sound. Those cowboys in the draw would be riding for help.

The shooting was still insistent, gun flashes coming from the draw, but there was a new regularity about it. Three or four guns were laying down the fire. That meant that those others were headed back for the ranch buildings.

She spurred away, urging the stallion to a run. After a mile across gently rising ground she turned sharply to the south and found concealment among fallen pillars of sand rock overlooking the draw. She swung down, struck the ground running, one hand dragging her Winchester from its saddle scabbard. She stood with one shoulder pressed against a wind-smoothed boulder. For a second she could hear nothing except wind and rain. Then other sounds became audible—distant shooting, a thunder of hoofs, and closer a clatter of horses up the draw's gravelly bottom.

She waited a while, Winchester poked through a cleft in the fallen boulders. The rock surface at her shoulder was dry, and heat of the afternoon sun still came from it. The seconds seemed long. For a quarter minute there had been no lightning. Too dark to see. She pointed in the general direction of approaching riders and pressed the trigger.

Concussion pounded hard from the rock faces. She moved to a new place, fired again. It was 100 to one against such blind bullets taking effect, and that suited her just as well. No point in doing more than frightening off these Mexican *vaqueros* and *gringo* cowboys that Millerick hired for forty a month.

Over the *whang* and echo of the Winchester she could hear them come to a clattering, sliding stop. She kept pumping the lever, moving from rock to rock. The barrel became hot in her hands.

Shooting back at her now. Four or five guns. A slug struck rock, powdering fragments that scorched the side of her face. For an instant the air was filled with the sulphurous smell of burned rock.

One of the men was shouting: "By damn, that's all the same gun! I'm a-goin' up thar!"

They were spurring up the steep side of the wash, circling on her from two directions. She swung back to the saddle. After almost half a minute of darkness, lightning came—a glowing zigzag wire that gave a long second of illumination. They saw her plainly trying to double back from the sand rocks.

A gun blazed. Its bullet roared closely. She turned the stallion and sent him plunging to the bottom of the wash. He half fell on the cutbank side. She was out of the saddle to prevent being pinned, but the horse wasn't hurt. He was up, still going, the girl clinging one foot in a stirrup, hand on the horn. She swung back to the saddle and gave him his head, trusting his eyes and instincts as he thundered down the crooked bottom.

Guns seemed to burst from all around her, webbing the night with flame, and a few seconds later they seemed far away, the twisting bottom of the dry wash hiding her from sight.

The cattle were gone now. Only a distant drum of their hoofs. She rode a couple of miles and met two of the *bandidos*. "Anyone hurt?" she asked.

"Not that we have seen, *señorita*," one of them answered.

"Lucio, by your voice."

"Yes, *señorita*."

"Who's with you?"

The *gringo*'s voice: "Me . . . Tucker."

She waited for him. "Good. You're better with a gun than most. You'd better stay behind . . . the two of you. Those riders will be getting help from the ranch. Delay them. I don't care how. We'll need time at the Río."

"Sure," Tucker drawled. "I'll blast their lights out."

"No need of killing."

"Say, you're a funny *bandido*, aren't you?"

"I said there was no need of killing. Drive them to cover, and keep on the move. Forget about the herd. Take the short road to Jacinto."

"Still planning on blasting El Gallo's?"

"Of course."

He laughed, the old, cynical jerk of his shoulders, but this time with a touch of admiration. "Lady, you'll end up queen of Méjico someday, or maybe we'll all end up dead."

She laughed at him. Something different about her tone. Some of the old defiance gone. Hard riding and shooting was like strong drink to her. She said—"*Adiós*."—and rode on, galloping, letting the stallion have his head.

Those wild longhorns ran almost as fast as horses, and they were strung out along the valley more than two miles ahead. Rimrocks would hold them there for a while, then the *bandidos* would have to swing them southwest, to Agua Frio, the only possible crossing in five miles that would escape cutbanks and mud.

Rain stopped, but thunder kept rolling along the horizon. The Río made a bright streak, cutting the darkness through broken, descending country below. Three of the *bandidos* were at the point, and the rest in swing positions, angling the herd down to Agua Frio, doing it easily enough now that the longhorns had run some of the orneriness from their slab sides.

For almost an hour there had been no gunfire, then it came again, a distant *crackle,* maybe a dozen shots. She rode to a rock knob and looked back along the stormy void without seeing gun flashes. Tucker and Lucio were far back, fighting their delaying action.

There would be time enough. Half an hour to cross the Río, and then the Jacinto close beyond. They'd be well out of sight when dawn came.

Lead steers where already belly deep in the Río when she rode forward to help direct the crossing. A bawling, milling mass had developed in mid-river with a couple dozen steers in the vortex but the river was not deep enough to drown many. *Bandidos* kept breaking the mass up, shouting, swinging *cuerdas* and rope goads, driving them up the Mexican side.

Rain had seemed like a cloudburst a while before, but it had formed less than an inch of mud and already hoofs had dug deep and were raising dust from the far bank. There was a level, low-water shelf along the shore, then a ten or twelve foot bank with willows edging it. Beyond were flats and the bare-rock approaches to Río Jacinto.

Laggard cattle were still crossing. No trouble. No ambush. It had been easy. The Ranger had been wrong. . . . Suddenly, from a dozen points, the night was laced with rifle fire.

Men had been waiting, concealed among willow and bank openings. The Apache was close ahead of The Angel. She saw him spin halfway around, one hand clutching his chest, the other clinging to the mane of his horse. A slug from the second volley hit him, driving him over backward, and he struck earth with arms flung widely. His horse was running, plunging wildly up the bank. A *bandido* toppled and was dragged by his plunging horse. They had been caught in the apex of crossfire. Others, more fortunate, were spurring away, covered by night and the mix-up of cattle.

The Winchester had been ready, lying across The Angel's saddle. She raised it, finger on the trigger, but for the moment she did not fire. Her stallion charged, pawing up the bank, ripped through a tangle of willows.

A man rose in front of her, rifle in his hands. Her Winchester exploded, smashing him down. His gun blazed almost straight in the air.

Other men were at her right and her left. She'd

ridden into a nest of them, but their surprise was as great as hers. One of the men went down beneath the stallion's hoofs. Burning powder whipped past. The man she'd ridden down was still alive, sending bullets screaming after her.

She could see cattle running in a dozen directions. No saving the herd. Everyone for himself now. The *bandidos* understood.

It was level going across the flats. She swung to the right, put the stallion up a steep pitch. A trail opened through rock pillars with the Jacinto's badland cliffs beyond. It was one that she often took, a short cut.

She eased back a trifle, slowing the stallion. There was still shooting from back by the river. Intermittent shots, clusters of them, and some-times quarter minute stretches of silence. No rain now, but water was still running hoof deep along a natural gutter formed by rock.

She heard a voice close in front of her: "Stop!"

It was El Gallo.

She sensed his movement and drove her spurs, but the stallion flung himself to one side. The animal was tangled in a reata that had been stretched across the trail. He went down, hoofs over head with the girl pitched face foremost. Rocks stunned her. She tried to move and couldn't. For the moment her body seemed congealed, useless.

El Gallo appeared, his huge form hunched. He

bent over, seized her wrist. Touch of his hand did something to her. She twisted, a cat-like movement, and her free hand went toward her gun.

El Gallo chuckled and trod her wrist underfoot. Then he reached and plucked the long-barreled gun from its holster.

She tried to fight free, but the man was too powerful. It was as though her wrist was held by a bear trap. His fingers closed harder and harder. He was laughing, enjoying this demonstration of his strength. All feeling had left her hand.

"Ho! So you see, *Señorita* Jaguar! Your Gallo is strong and queek, and sharp of mind, too."

She stopped fighting and let him drag her upright. He got hold of her other wrist, drew her arms straight to her sides. His massive face was grinning, pressed close to hers. He'd prepared himself for the meeting. He'd perfumed himself, pomaded his moustaches which were tied beneath his chin with bright new ribbon.

"You . . . hurt me," she whispered.

"Ho. So now you sound like woman. Thus at last you learn that you cannot fight your Gallo. At last you . . ."

She'd made a pretense of surrender, then she bent with a darting, feline movement to sink teeth in his wrist. But El Gallo had learned his lesson with her. He let go with that hand, flung her out, let her crack at the end of the other arm as though he were snapping a whip. Her sombrero flew from her head, struck stones with a *jingle* of silver ornaments.

"Ho! So will your El Gallo teach you who is master. Like he teach high-spirit horse." He changed hands and snapped her once again. And again. Her scrap of mantilla had been dislodged and was around her throat, her mask half off. Her hair had come free and was cascaded in stray-colored masses over her shoulders. He stopped, bent, and ripped off her mask the rest of the way.

Then he crouched, peering down at her. Dully, from the nightmare of her half-consciousness she could hear his voice,

"So. As El Gallo think. It is you, the proud *Señorita* Torretagles. You will be fine woman for El Gallo. A fine woman for sit at El Gallo's table when he teach you who is master."

# IX

She had no clear recollection of mounting the stallion, but she was in the saddle, her hands free, and feet tied with rawhide thongs to the stirrups. It was night, with a hint of storm still in the air. She glanced around and saw El Gallo, huge, hunched forward on his mustang. A bit of plaited rawhide reata ran from his saddle to the stallion's bridle. Her hand instinctively went to her waist, but the gun was gone.

"No, *Señorita* Torretagles," El Gallo said. "I have taken it. You can do nothing. Only to come. It will be easier if you learn who is master now."

They crossed the Río Jacinto's mile-wide bottom, took some switchbacks up a steep arroyo side, over a ridge, across cliffs and wild talus slopes. Dawn came up, silhouetting the jagged horizon. They rode to a rock shelf overhanging a cliff, and there El Gallo drew in and pointed down.

"Behold, *señorita*! See now the hiding place your Gallo has got you."

Almost directly below, lying in the closed end of a blind cañon, was an adobe cabin, a couple of sheds, some mesquite corrals, small shanties.

He went on talking: "When El Gallo train horse, he do not want others to watch. Thees is not good for pride of fine horse. So with women. You, I bring here. No man can tell El Gallo of horse or women."

She looked at him, eyes showing no fear. Only contempt.

"You do not fear? Ho! It is true that one of noble Torretagles blood would not fear. But you have yet to learn what sort of man your Gallo is."

He nudged the mustang and moved on, leading the stallion across one ledge to another, descending in a series of little steps, many of them drilled and blasted from the rock. The trail fell away, and in its place was a bridge of wooden slabs suspended from above by ropes. Beyond they entered slide rock, and then the bottoms and the head box of a spring.

Half a dozen mustangs were inside a corral, but no man showed himself.

"Pablo!" El Gallo called. "Pablo, you hear me?"

No one answered. The wild mustangs took fright and their hoofs flung dirt as they milled in the small circle of the corral.

"Pablo! Damn you to sleep when El Gallo say watch!" There was a long adobe shed beyond the corrals, and El Gallo paused to peer through the door. Two saddles hung on a rack. He grunted and swung around, letting his narrowed eyes sweep the cañon. "Pablo! Answer me, *Señor* Jackass! Ha! So *Señor* Jackass is disobey El Gallo." He looked over at the girl. "Do you know what El Gallo do with men who disobey him?"

"You kill them," she answered in an uninterested voice.

"So. El Gallo keel them." He leveled one thick forefinger. "Bang! Through belly he keel them."

He went on, keeping the mustang at a slow jog, his *peso*-rowelled spurs *jingling,* and drew up in front of a thick-walled adobe cabin. He sat for a while looking at the half-closed door, then he swung down and walked with his fancy, braid-bordered pants sticking to the insides of his bowed legs and booted it open. Dawn was bright now and enough light entered the tiny windows for him to see a rough board table, a fireplace with its big iron kettle on a hook, some pole and slab chairs, a double bunk against the far wall covered with dirty quilts. The scrutiny seemed to satisfy him.

He came back, drawing the Bowie from its sheath at the back of his neck and cut the thongs holding her feet. His left hand had closed on her right wrist. As she dismounted, he drew a rawhide quirt from the band of his pants.

"You used *cuerda* one night on El Gallo. Now perhaps is his turn. Do not tempt me, *señorita.* Go inside!"

She did not move, and with a powerful swing of his shoulders he flung her, sending her sprawling inside, across the dirt floor. He strode after her. She was sitting, propped on one hand, one leg doubled under her. Not looking at him. Her eyes were on something at one side of the door. El Gallo started to close the door, noticed the direction of her gaze.

He turned. The quirt dropped from his fingers in momentary surprise. There, seated on a puncheon stool, back against the wall, was Millerick. Millerick was smiling, and a six-shooter was in his hand, cocked and pointed.

"El Gallo!" he said in his high-pitched voice. "I've been expecting you."

El Gallo said something, identity of the words lost in his heavy throat. He backed away a step. He crouched, long arms swinging, fingertips resting on the bagged-out knees of his pants.

Millerick went on: "You had an idea of fooling me, didn't you? Ambush our Angel, and take the cattle for yourself."

"No, *gringo*. El Gallo keep hees word. El Gallo only . . ."

"No use, Gallo." Millerick watched the girl get up and a smug smile touched his lips. "I didn't expect you to be bringing The Angel herself. Or should I call her Camila Torretagles?"

El Gallo had recovered sufficiently to swagger a little. He commenced to laugh. "Oh, ho! Ho-ho-ho!" He placed hands on hips and roared in bursts, each one louder and longer than the last. "Thees is joke. On you is joke. You, the wise, the smart *gringo* so clever as ride into El Gallo's cabin to ambush him. But what about El Gallo's men? You think he does not have men here? Even now are El Gallo's men outside ready to keel you if you but pull trigger."

"Two of your men are here."

"Eh?"

"Two of them. They're both dead."

Light coming through the small cleft window struck El Gallo's forehead showing the glisten of perspiration. His thick lips were open a little, and the moustaches, pulling on the upper one, made it roll out in an idiotic manner. He was staring, gaze fixed on the six-shooter in Millerick's hand as it came up little by little with its sights centering on his heart.

Millerick said softly: "So that only leaves you, Gallo."

"No! Not to shoot! Hear me. El Gallo is most powerful *bandido* on border. Tomorrow no one in Chihuahua will stand in front of him. Then will he do business with *gringo* rancher. Then will he . . ."

The muscles of Millerick's hand had gone tense. El Gallo ceased talking, eyes staring at the trigger finger. He knew it was coming and the moment of waiting seemed very long. The gun exploded, smashing lead and flame across the little room. The slug struck El Gallo in the chest. He reeled back on bowed legs, arms lifted shoulder high. His back and head struck the adobe wall; he rebounded. Fingers tore at his uniform tunic. The gun exploded again, and he spun sidewise, took a step going down, and ended head foremost against the far wall.

Millerick stood up. Black powder smoke filled the room, making it hard to see. He coughed from the fumes, walked to the man, stood over him. He reached with one excellently wrought boot and nudged him. El Gallo was dead.

The girl watched, eyes fixed on the fallen man. Not in terror, but repugnance. She looked over and met Millerick's eyes and her expression did not change.

He said: "You see? I'm not such a bad fellow, after all. You hadn't fooled me with your disguise. I knew all along that you were The Angel. And yet, after everything, I've come here and saved you."

Boots crunched the rocky path outside and a rangy, raw-boned man in cowboy clothes stood with a six-shooter drawn, looking inside.

"All right, boss?"

"Yes, everything's all right."

The man looked over, saw The Angel, and grinned. He had a cruel face, large-beaked, with a deep cleft scar across his right cheek pulling it out of shape. "What now, boss? Think there'll be more of them?"

"Go back to your post," Millerick piped. Then, when the man started away: "Shicora! Don't let any of them get this far."

"I know how to take care of greasers."

Shicora had left the door open. Millerick backed against it, closing it with his shoulders. A bar of heavy, twisted mesquite wood leaned against the wall. He hoisted it, dropped it into place.

"You can't keep me here," she said.

Millerick laughed. "It's for your own safety. There might be shooting downcañon before the morning's over. These adobe walls are thick. They'll stop bullets." He was talking quietly, with pretended courtesy, but the smile on his lips made the words sound venomous. He took a step toward her as she backed away. "Girl, don't look at me like that. A person would almost think you'd prefer El Gallo."

"I would prefer El Gallo!"

She meant it, and the certainty that she meant it was a jilt to Millerick. He was the sort of man who could spend hours looking at himself in the mirror, and it had always mystified him that others did not find him equally attractive. But the girl's tone had left no doubt. She detested him.

Millerick's lips thinned, showing just the tips of his perfectly formed teeth. He was tall. Standing full height in his high-heeled boots, his sombrero almost scraped the ceiling. He took one stride, another. Her eyes were shifting and alert. Suddenly she bent double, dodged forward.

The quickness of it almost eluded him. His hand swung down, seized her forearm. He expected her to twist aside, perhaps go to the floor. Instead, she moved close and the impact of her body made him fall back half a step. Her hand found one of his ivory-handled Colt pistols and was pulling it from its holster.

He let her go, and swung one hand, chopping the gun to the floor. She dropped, trying to recover it. He booted it across the room.

She was free now. Her eyes spied the quirt that El Gallo had dropped. She grabbed it, spun, and ripped its lash across Millerick's face.

He was blinded for a moment, one hand flung in front of his eyes. The lash cut him again. He charged, carrying her against the wall. Ripped the quirt from her fingers.

She was like a mountain cat, fighting him away. Her teeth were bared, her nails slashing his flesh.

He tried to force her against the wall and use his weight to overpower her. The savagery of her defense blinded him, made him stagger back. Then, cursing, he swung the heel of his palm, catching her between neck and jaw. It was a brutal blow. Her head snapped back, striking the adobe wall. She pitched forward and was on her knees, eyes baffled, lacking direction. Millerick paused, fingering hair from eyes. He rubbed his face, looked at his palm thick with blood.

She was trying to get up. He reached down, seized her knotted hair, dragged her to her feet, and struck her again. This time he did not let her fall. He held her by her upper arms.

"You . . . The Angel!" he hissed. "La Hija de Satanás! That's who you'd rather be. Masked, with your hair rolled under your hat, a gun at your waist, and a *cuerda* coiled in your hand. A devil. You'd rather be those things than a woman and take the best that a good man like myself had to offer you. My name. The honor of being my wife." He shook her back and forth. Her hair was coming down and he shook her the harder until it strung in curling, brown masses over her shoulders. "There," he hissed. "Like that. That's how you were meant to be a woman."

He took her in his arms. She fought him, but he drew her close. Her *chaleco* and black silk shirt had pulled away, revealing part of one white breast. He pressed his lips there and took them away, leaving a smear of blood.

"Woman! In the name of the devil, don't you realize that you still could wind me around your finger."

Guns were hammering outside, bounding and rebounding from the sheer cañon walls. Seconds passed before Millerick seemed to hear them, then he lifted his head like one awakening.

Boots grated the path, running to the door. A fist was hammering. Shicora was shouting outside: "Millerick!"

"What is it?" Millerick snarled back. ". . . That shooting?"

"It looks like The Angel's *bandido* gang."

"How many?"

"Eight . . . ten."

"You can handle them, can't you?"

"Sure I can handle them."

"That's what I'm hiring you for!" He held the girl at arm's length and looked at her. "Your *bandidos*! We expected El Gallo's men, but it can just as well be these!"

There were a couple of times during the thunder and deluge when Tom Garrett might have broken

130

away from old Esteban and ridden to safety, but he did not make the move. It was too late for him to stop the girl from raiding those Millerick cattle, and the prospect of meeting her at some *bandido* rendezvous later was not wholly unattractive. So he rode peacefully, keeping his mustang just ahead of Esteban as they crossed the Río and entered the deep cut of Jacinto.

Esteban kept going at a steady pace as the Jacinto became progressively wilder, its size magnified by darkness. He seemed to know every cliff and mesa, every crazy-crooked cañon. A rock trail led to sheltering cliffs and inside a natural cavern filled with stale horse and camp smells.

There he swung down and said: "It is dark, *gringo*, but I see well enough. We will wait here."

"For how long?"

"*¿Quién sabe?*" His teeth could be seen in the dark as he griped: "For you, perhaps, always."

Garrett hunkered on his boot heels, smoking hand-rolled cigarettes one after another. Dawn commenced finding its way along the horizon, lighting the cavern. There was considerable horse sign around, and the rock ceiling had been sooted over by numerous campfires. It was one of their usual meeting places.

Old Esteban took no chances. Not once did he re-holster the six-shooter or turn his back. Hoofs could be heard from a considerable distance, their sound caught by the cavern door, and he stood, the side of his face toward Garrett, watching for the better part of five minutes before the men showed themselves.

Six of them strung into sight, one after another. Light was behind them, making it hard to see their faces, but they were all tired and mud-spattered.

"Hello, Ranger!" a familiar voice said. It was Tucker, the outlaw. He swung down, looking lean and vicious. "What in the devil are *you* doing here?"

"The Angel sent me. I thought you knew."

"She has Rangers riding for her these days?"

Esteban said: "She caught him in lie back by creek at Block M. He said perhaps Millerick ambush. Maybe when she come . . ." He ended by pointing the six-shooter and pantomiming a shot.

"Oh, no, Esteban. That shows how damned little you know about women." Tucker grinned with half his face and spat the sodden remains of his cigarette. He said to Garrett: "She's taken a fancy to you, hasn't she?"

"Me?" Garrett stood, looking into Tucker's narrowed eyes.

"Sure, you. And for that I'd like to put a slug right through your guts. There's no reason for me liking you. You ran me out of Texas. You and your kind. You'd swing me from a cottonwood right this morning if you caught me on the other side of the Río and got the drop. Well, you're here, on

132

this side of the Río. My side. Sauce for the gander, hey? I ought to do it."

"But you won't."

"No, I won't. And do you know why? Because I don't want that gal to slice my head off with her *cuerda*."

"Where is she?"

"I wish I knew. They were laying for us at the Río. I wasn't along. She's disappeared."

"Millericks's ambush."

"No. El Gallo. I saw a couple dead ones when I rode by, and they were both Gallo's men. Strange thing, it was on the Mex side."

"After the cattle crossed?"

"Sure, afterward."

"He double-crossed Millerick, then."

Another *bandido* came. His left arm was ripped by a flesh wound. Carlos—a big, heavy-faced Mexican Indian.

"*Sí*. El Gallo," he muttered, making a face from pain as he tried to open and close the hand. "Eet was El Gallo. He eet was and these eyes saw him een Río Jacinto, by flash of lightning, riding away with The Angel."

"With The Angel?" Tucker strode towards him. "You say she was with El Gallo?"

"*Sí*. Weeth him. I saw . . . two horse. Big stallion. I know that devil horse anywhere. And mustang with lead rope. He take her uptrail."

"And what did you do?"

"With wounded arm, *señor*?"

"You let him take her without a fight?"

Carlos backed away from him, his hand groping back, jerking at the pistol at his hip. He'd rammed it in the holster too hard. He managed to draw the thing, but a *bandido* grabbed him from behind, and just in time to save his life, for, with a smooth, quick grab, Tucker had drawn. He checked himself short of shooting, the barrel tilted up.

"You let him take her?" he repeated.

"She was able to care for herself, no? Weeth *cuerda* she beat you from horse. Ees she not then . . . ?"

Tucker called him something and turned away. He stood, looking around at mud-streaked, tired faces.

Garrett broke the moment of silence: "If one of you lads would lend me a gun . . ."

Tucker spun on him. "Sure. You're damned right I'll lend you a gun. And I'll ride with you, too, if you have it on your mind to gun for El Gallo. I'd stack two rabble soldiers like us against any twelve of the toughest Mex between here and Chihuahua."

Esteban cried: "Someday perhaps I will keel you for this insult, *gringo*, but not today! Today I ride along. Today we all ride along. We will show you how Mexican *bandido* shoot."

There were eight of them when they started,

only the wounded Carlos staying behind. It was Esteban who led the way, following a trail through the manzanita that hid the cave mouth, climbing cliffs to a rim, crossing the heaped rocks of a summit with 1,000 square miles of twisted country stretching away to nowhere.

# X

A shot sounded as they neared El Gallo's. They rode to a flat ledge overlooking the closed end of a cañon, the circular area of flat ground crowded with sheds, corrals, an adobe house. A dozen mustangs were in the corral, their ears up, showing that something was going on. Outside the enclosure were two saddled horses picking at green grass bordering a spring hole. One was The Angel's black stallion, the other a mustang.

As they watched, a man came in view, moving with long strides downcañon from the adobe house. There were other buildings in that direction.

Garrett made a surprised movement and turned to Tucker: "Recognize him?"

"No."

"That's Shicora."

"Jib Shicora?" He peered down with no interest, but the man was just passing from view. "What's that killer doing here?"

"Millerick's man."

Garrett dismounted, walked down the ledge on foot. He returned a few seconds later with the muscles of his jaw set and eyes narrowed, and remounted.

"Bad?" asked Tucker.

"Suicide trail. One man with a Winchester could blast the gang of us." He looked at Esteban. "Isn't there another way?"

"There's a trail from downcañon. Narrow. Bad." He smiled contemptuously. "*Gringo* afraid of some little shooting?"

Garrett said: "You get your boys down on that lower trail. I don't care what you do as long as you raise plenty of hell. There might be one man down in those shacks, and there might be fifty. Cut loose and keep them busy. I have an idea it's just about a two-man job from this end." He looked over at Tucker. "Ever wonder how the ducks feel in a shooting gallery?"

Tucker laughed, twisted up a cigarette, lit it. The cigarette jerked up and down in the scissored corner of his mouth when he answered: "In this shooting gallery the ducks are likely to shoot back."

They watched Esteban lead his *bandidos* around the cliff rim, took time to go over their guns. Tucker was carrying two six-shooters and a Winchester in a saddlebag. He drew out the Winchester, laid it across the pommel. Garrett had recovered his guns from Esteban, and he preferred the Winchester in his hands, too.

Tucker asked: "How long will it take Esteban?"

"He didn't say. Five minutes, maybe. You can see a few chunks of the lower trail down there a quarter mile."

It was hard just sitting, waiting. The *bandido* mustangs kept making noise as they moved along the rocky cañon rim, but so far nobody noticed from below.

Men were talking. American voices. They were 100 paces away, but whole groups of words could be understood.

"Not El Gallo's men," Tucker said. "You suppose Carlos made a mistake and Millerick's riding with her instead . . . ?"

"Nobody could mistake Millerick for El Gallo."

A rifle shot shattered the dawn quiet, rocking from one rock wall to another, and leaving a few seconds of ringing silence.

Too soon for Esteban to make it down the cañon trail, but there was no time to speculate. Garrett touched spurs to his mustang and started down, keeping him at a trot down the unfamiliar trail, moving from ledge to ledge. There was a switchback that placed them in full view of the buildings below. A half dozen men were in sight, moving among the adobe buildings, ducking from rock to rock.

Esteban had evidently decided against trying the lower trail. His men had left the horses and were shooting down from the rugged cañon rocks.

137

He was keeping them busy. One of Millerick's gunmen was face down with his arms flung out, a nickel-plated revolver making a bright shine by rising sunlight. For the moment none of them noticed the two riders descending the trail at their backs.

The trail became narrow. It was hand cut from the cliff. Then the soft streak of a slide where the trail ended and in its place was a bridge of mesquite slate rawhided together at the outer ends, suspended from above by an intricate series of ropes.

Garrett's mustang stopped short, its legs braced. He cursed, lashed it, drove his spurs. The mustang wheeled short and tried to climb the cliff wall. He was about to go over backward. Garrett rolled from the saddle, landed, half falling, with the Winchester under one arm, sprang forward, and ran, crouching, over the swaying suspension bridge.

Tucker's mustang couldn't get by. The two of them were threatening to drive each other into the abyss. Garrett's got by somehow and galloped back up the steep trail.

Tucker had dismounted and was following. He glimpsed the two men above, wheeled, tossed the gun to his shoulder. Garrett dived face foremost across the last few feet of the bridge. Shicora's gun *whanged,* its bullet tearing rock fragments and droning away.

Garrett had landed on elbows, the carbine in

both hands. For a second he was beyond Shicora's view. Tucker still up, crouched far over. He pitched, face down, ending in the angle between trail and cliff.

Garrett drew himself forward from elbow to elbow, belly down, the rifle in front of him. He raised, but Shicora wasn't where he expected. Two other men had appeared from nowhere. One of them carried a heavy Henry rifle and the sun, just rising, raised a flat shine from one octagonal face of its barrel. The other man was holding a six-shooter.

The one with the Henry gun was peering up at the trail, gun half lifted to his shoulder. He glimpsed Garrett's movement, tossed the gun to his shoulder. Garrett fired. A snap shot without using sights, but the range was not long. Fifty yards. The slug struck the man and drove him back with arms wrapped around his middle. The man with the Colt was clawing for cover with Tucker raising geysers of dirt behind his heels, past his shoulders. From farther downcañon somebody was shooting, hammering rock fragments, ripping splinters from the bridge.

"We have fifteen seconds," Tucker said.

Garrett nodded, knowing what he meant. They were safe only till Shicora or his men could move along the cañon wall and reach the adobe buildings farther down. After that they'd have little chance on the slanting ledge.

Garrett twisted over, looked at the trail's ledge. Slabs of mesquite had been placed there, wedged with rock, partly to secure the bridge, partly as a retaining wall. It gave him three or four inches of concealment from the side but would expose him if he tried it over the edge.

He noticed that Tucker had pulled himself to one knee. He was clinging to the wall with one hand, the other wrapped across his chest. He'd been hit; blood had soaked through his faded blue shirt and was running across his hands, bright scarlet by early sunshine.

"You're hit."

"Hit be damned. This is raspberry pop. Get the hell over the edge. It's your only chance."

"Come along! I . . ."

Tucker cursed him. "Get over the edge. I'll cover you from up here. What the hell? I got nothing to lose."

Garrett raised to see what chance he had if he jumped. There was a thirty-foot drop with block slabs of rock heaped below. No time to hesitate. Tucker had lifted his carbine again and was pumping the lever, sending a stream of bullets into the adobe houses, trying to drive Millerick's men down. Garrett swung over the edge, clung for a second by one hand, and dropped feet first.

Half a dozen bullets ripped around him, but the rough face of the cliff gave a measure of protection. It was not perpendicular. More like eighty degrees, and there were uneven, earthy spots where mesquite had taken root and grew in dwarf clumps, hanging by wire-tough roots.

He hit bottom with rocks and dirt showering him. Rocks on both sides gave concealment. The Winchester was still in his left hand. He took time to stuff cartridges in the magazine, glanced to make sure that the muzzle was free of dirt.

They'd be watching for his first appearance, so he circled, kept down among the rocks. They blocked his vision as well as hiding him. He had to reconstruct the layout from memory. At one side was the spring box and the circular corrals. Joining the corrals was a long, brush-roofed shed, and that led directly to the adobe house.

The rocks played out and he ran across the open separating him from corrals. Bullets followed, pounding the earth as he flung himself belly down and slid through the lower poles of the corral. Frightened mustangs were swirling around, tossing their unroached manes.

He remained on one knee a few seconds, getting his breath. Then he looked around, appraising his position. He wasn't as well off as he had expected. The corral was built in a circle. He was at its farthest bulge, for the moment hidden by two upright posts. In crossing to the shed he'd place himself in full view of those guns down the cañon. Even so, he'd have a fifty-fifty chance if all of them were on the ground like himself, but by this time one or more might have a place of vantage on the roof.

The mustangs were bunched at the far side, watching him, nostrils distended, flanks quivering. He took off his hat and flagged it to the ground. They were off on a wild swing around the corral, hoofs flinging dirt and manure. For a second or two they were between him and the guns. He crossed, drawing not a shot, and entered the long, low shed.

The place was dim and cool, filled with the odors of horses and harness leather. Some bunks were built in what had once been a box stall and the walls were covered with steel engravings of pretty girls. Just in front of the box stall lay a dead man, face down. He'd been shot in the back, running, when the bullet hit him. Garrett turned him over. He was one of the *bandidos* that had accompanied El Gallo that night in the *cantina*. Dead about an hour.

Garrett commenced to string it all together then. El Gallo had evidently double-crossed Millerick by giving no warning of The Angel's raid. That's why there was no full crew at the Block M watching the beef herd. Then Gallo, with an eye to getting the herd for himself, had laid his own ambush across the Río. But Millerick was one jump ahead. No doubt he had a spy in El Gallo's ranks. At any rate he'd been here awaiting the *bandido* chief's return. In that case, it was probably Millerick in the cabin.

He stood up, and walked along the shed pausing at its front door. Only a dozen strides separated him from the cabin. Its door, however, was on the far side and it would be suicide reaching it. His only chance was a window about breast height from the ground, no more than two and a half feet square. No glass. Only a covering of deer skin, scraped, oiled, and turned translucent from age. The skin had been pegged to the rough pole window casing, and a man would need a knife to cut through.

He felt his pockets, drew a clasp knife, opened the large blade with his teeth, slid it under his belt. Then he stepped out into the bright sunshine.

He expected a bullet from somewhere—any-where. Only the steady shooting from downcañon. He glanced above at the trail and suspension bridge, but of course there was no sign of Tucker. He couldn't remember hearing a gun from that direction, so probably the wound had finished him. Esteban and his *bandidos* seemed to be getting in their licks from overhead.

He reached the wall, stood by the window. He could hear movement inside, and Millerick's voice.

"You're being a fool," he was saying in his womanish tone. "If you expect those bandits to fight their way through . . ."

"Stay away from me," came the girl's voice.

Millerick laughed. "Yes, I know you hate me.

143

But I'm past caring about that. I'm ready to take what I want."

He could tell that the man was holding her, and that she was struggling to free herself. He drew the knife, thrust the blade through the lower corner of the skin window, made a slice along the bottom and up the side. It still hung across the window. He could hear the girl breathing through her nostrils, the laugh in Millericks's voice as he went on talking to her, asserting his strength.

"You're strong, aren't you?" he was saying. "Strong. . . ."

Garrett boosted himself to the edge, swung the knife once again, cutting the skin across the top, and it fell away, revealing him there.

Inside was a well of flickering darkness after the brilliant morning sunshine. He had only a vague impression of movement, heard the girl's cry as Millerick spun around. He dived from the sill. At the last instant he caught an impression of Millerick's form and changed direction. He slammed the man waist high, carrying him to a wall. They struck and rebounded. Millerick ripped himself to one side, freeing one hand, going for his right-hand gun.

Garrett had no time to get the Colt on his own hip. He knew that Millerick had drawn, was trying to bring the gun up between them, pull the trigger. A bullet through Garrett's groin or even his leg would do the business. Those .44s will put a man down no matter where they hit him.

144

Garrett's hand darted down, closed on Millerick's wrist. He rammed it wide. The gun exploded, lashing lead and burning powder to the floor.

They reeled across the room. Millerick was powerful, heavy, angry, but for the moment no advantage went to him. A stool tangled them and they trod over it, shattering it. Suddenly Millerick bent double and came up, twisting Garrett's arm over his head.

It was a good trick. A whip lock, designed to twist the arm out of joint at the shoulder and stretch him full length across the floor. Garrett managed to pull free. Millerick tried to swing the gun on him. They were too close. Instead, he swung the barrel to Garrett's skull.

Garrett tried to spin aside. He moved enough to save a crushed skull. The glancing blow was like an explosion in his eardrums and the dim room burst into yellow and blue lights. The floor was there to meet him. He forced himself to hands and knees. His veins seemed to be filled with molten lead making every movement heavy and slow. He fumbled for his gun. The holster had twisted over, spilling it out. He knew that Millerick was above him. He expected a bullet in the brain.

But the girl had screamed something and pounced on Millerick's arm. Her unexpected ferocity and strength forced his arm wide, and his finger accidentally squeezed the trigger, firing a bullet that hammered chunks from the adobe wall.

She clung with a wild animal strength. Millerick's womanish voice rose in a shrill scream of rage. He braced his legs and hurled her with all the massive strength of his body.

She was torn free, sent flying across the room. She struck the adobe wall and went down, stunned, sitting, one leg bent under her, head forward, hair falling in masses over her lap.

Garrett reeled to his feet. It seemed to take him a long time, but actually only while Millerick wheeled back with the gun. Garrett's ears still buzzed, but he was young, with a youthful resilience that was sending the old quickness back in his muscles.

He thrust the gun away with an outflung left hand, set himself, heels wide on the dirt floor, and smashed a right to Millerick's jaw. Millerick saw the blow coming and at the final instant tried to block it off. Too late. It struck fully on his jaw, snapping his head back. The gun was still in his hand. He pulled the trigger blindly as he reeled back. Explosion was deafening in the tiny room, the air blue from powder smoke.

Garrett struck him again. The man reeled, the back of his head striking the wall. His gun slipped, struck his knee, bounded away. He tried to recover it, remembered he had a second gun, reached. Garrett struck him again.

His eyes were off focus. His mouth dropped open with blood running from the corners.

Nothing handsome about him now. His face was repulsive from terror.

"No, Garrett," he whispered. "No. I'm through. Let me go, Garrett. I'll take my boys. Over the Río. That's for sure. Take my boys . . ."

He was holding himself up with one hand braced on the wall. Hair filled with sweat and adobe dust was strung over his face. His left hand groped for the other gun while he was asking for mercy.

Garrett let a contemptuous laugh jerk his shoulders, shifted his feet a trifle, and smashed Millerick again. His head rocked as though striking the end of a hangman's rope. Sweat snapped from his hair. He went down, legs doubled under him. He was still feeling for the left-hand gun. The barrel was pinched under him and it came out hard. Garrett waited for a second and kicked it from his hand.

Light from the window was suddenly cut off. Garrett spun around. It was the gunman, Shicora. He stood, big, raw-boned, and scar-faced, a six-shooter laid across the bottom sill.

It took Shicora's eyes a moment to pierce the dimness and powder smoke, then he located Garrett and his lips twisted in sort of a grin.

"Turn around and take it in the breast, Ranger. That's how a man should take his last bullet."

Garrett fell back a step. No gun in his holster— he remembered that. It was on the ground a step away. No chance of reaching it. Only a touch of Shicora's finger was needed to blast the life out of him.

Millerick was on his knees, fingering hair and blood from his face. He saw Shicora, the gun, and realization came. He laughed, a sudden wild sound with his treble voice.

"Shicora! Good old Shicora. Shoot him low, Shicora. Let him kick for a while, Shicora."

"No, boss. Not for Shicora. I always like to do a nice, clean job. Through the heart."

His finger tensed on the trigger, but something hit him, spinning him to one side. The *crash* of a Winchester came a fragment of time later. Sound of it seemed impersonal through the thick, dirt wall.

The high-speed bullet had smashed cleanly through Shicora's left shoulder, down through his chest, and emerged to pound dirt fragments from the window. His eyes were open, staring, six-gun dangling limply in his fingers. With eyes still looking straight ahead he slipped backward to the ground.

Garrett knew. It was Tucker, still cached on the cliff trail.

Millerick seemed stunned for an instant. Then he sprang toward one of the ivory-handled six-shooters. He seized it, twisted around, crouched. Garrett had anticipated the move. He took one long stride, snatched up his .44, and fired.

Millerick went back as though hit by a sledge. His gun was in his hand, cocked, but there was no life left in him to pull the trigger. Tension went out of him and he lay still on the dirt floor.

Garrett strode over, looked down on him. He was dead.

He turned, flung open the door. Men were escaping on foot up the steep, southern wall. Millerick's gunmen. A nest of them still cached by the adobe barn were putting up a defensive fire while *bandidos* edged closer.

He saw Tucker coming down the cliff trail, one arm dangling from the bullet wound in his shoulder.

He saw Garrett and asked: "Where is she?"

"She's all right."

"Millerick?"

"And El Gallo. I'll lay dollars to *pesos* Millerick 'bushed him. Maybe I'll end up the *bandido* chief of the border. Unless you'd rather go back to the States. I think I . . ."

"The hell with you. I might fight beside a Ranger, but I'd never trust one north of the Río." He sat down, shoulder against a rock, ignoring the downcañon shooting, let the Winchester lay across his knees. He fished for tobacco and papers, rolled a cigarette, sat with it clenched in his thin mouth. "You Rangers are all alike. You're not human. You'd snap my neck tomorrow if you caught me in Texas."

Garrett laughed with something like his old, easy good nature and went back inside.

Camila Torretagles had risen and was holding the wall for support. She was still dizzy from the blow she had taken. She made no resistance when Garrett slipped an arm around her waist to support her. She seemed content to remain there, cheek pressed against the rough cloth of his shirt, her hair falling in ringlet masses over his chest.

"There's still shooting outside," she whispered.

"Your *bandidos*. They seem to be first-class fighting men."

"My *bandidos* no longer," she whispered. "From today I am only Camila Torretagles. It would be better that way."

She looked up, lips parted, smiling a little. Her midnight blue eyes were looking at him. It was the first he'd noticed their peculiar color. He'd seen eyes like that before in the mingling of the north European and Latin races.

He knew she was waiting for him to kiss her. "Camila Torretagles," he said. "Yes, that would be better. I'd like Missus Tom Garrett even better."

"Perhaps," she whispered, "it could be arranged."

# Two Queens
# for Skidway Empire

# I

Buzz Leary stopped for a few seconds, blocking the steps of the beat-up passenger coach, and from that vantage point had a look at Red Bank. It wasn't much like the Red Bank he remembered from five years ago. Then it had been a settlement; now it was a booming railroad construction camp rising, false-fronted and tent-roofed, from quagmire streets. Only the hills were the same, the limitless hill and forest country of British Columbia, great-chested, rising toward the distant, ice-blocked summits of the High Caribou.

Leary took a deep breath. The air was sharp and forest-scented. It struck his body like alcohol, took the sluggishness from it, placed a tingle in his muscles. Men behind him, trying to get off, were packed tightly. They were shouting at him. The huge Swedish construction worker at his back finally lost patience, and bellowing—"Har, noo!"—charged, shoulder first, with weight and a momentum that sent Leary staggering. He stayed up for two steps, then sprawled across the rough-plank depot platform.

Leary rolled to his feet, leaving his war bag where he'd dropped it. He was taller than the Swede, a rangy 170, but the Swede outweighed him by thirty pounds. Leary was poised with his fists ready, but the Swede tossed up both hands.

"Yumpin yimminy, Ay can't fight wit'out chew snooce."

Buzz Leary laughed and said: "To hell with you. You'll get no snooce from me. It'll ruin your health. But I'll buy you a shot of moose milk."

The Swede linked his arm and they crossed the jam-packed depot station platform with smaller men getting out of their way. A moment later they were over the high heels of their logger boots in muck.

For a while, Leary had forgotten about the Neil boys, but there, with the main street in front of him, he looked for them. It occurred to him that he should have taken his .38 Colt double-action out of the war bag and placed it in some friendlier spot. Inside his Mackinaw, for instance. Just in case the Neil boys took a timber-wolf view of his return. Then he said: "To hell with 'em!"

"Yah," the big Swede said, without knowing what he was talking about. "To hell wit' 'em. You show me a Norwegian and Ay skol a cemetery."

They walked into the first saloon they came to. Leary had two drinks while the Swede was having four. The saloon was a little keg-and-tincup affair with frame sides and a canvas roof. A stove flamed hot from a load of pitch knots and the heat, combined with whiskey on an empty stomach, made him lose the keen edge of his faculties. He'd need them if he ran into the Neils.

He tossed his war bag to his shoulder and left the Swede doing a noisy schottische on his hobnails, and singing:

> My name it bane Swanson
> Ay come from Wisconsin
> To work in the timber land
> Bane ride to Shee-boygin
> On Yim Hill's red wagon
> Wit' axe handle in my hand.

Outside, following the corduroy sidewalks, Leary could still hear him as he stamped his hobs and bellowed the chorus of the timber-jack song:

> Ay wear a red collar,
> Ay drink saxteen dollar,
> Wit' axe handle in my hand.

A big, ramshackle building that had been the general warehouse and office of the Red Bank Lumber Company now bore a sign reading Rocky Mountain Hotel. Leary walked toward it. With the war bag on his shoulders, he looked taller than his six foot one. It broadened the apparent width of his shoulders. His was of a build one often saw among the timber stiffs of the Pacific slope. His face as well as his body showed strength. He might even have been handsome in an untamed way if it hadn't been for a nose, twice broken and badly knit, and for a right cheek that was puckered from a series of parallel hobnail scars.

The lobby was dim. Leary paused. There was a bleary old man behind the desk; near the window sat a girl almost hidden by an Edmonton newspaper. She wore a tight whipcord dress, and her posture, with one knee over the other, her slim body bent aside to catch the light, made him want to see the rest of her. Just then she dropped the paper and looked at him over it. He could see her eyes. They were dark and lovely. Then the paper hid them, and he walked on to the desk, saying: "I need a room."

The clerk waggled his gray head and said: "You timber stiffs better have your own balloon and nosebag when you hit these railroad camps. What rooms we got are for the boiled-collar boys. We ain't even got a stray bed. Have to roll your soogins in the bullpen. Two dollars."

Leary tossed his war bag behind the counter, with the .38 too close to the side making a heavy *thud*. He watched the clerk, but the old man didn't seem to notice.

"How can you get downriver to Skidway?" Leary asked.

"Railroad barge. Tell 'em you're a shovel punk and you can ride free." He was more friendly after getting Leary's $2. "You looking for a job in the woods? Come around next year. Things will be poppin' in this country once the railroad goes through."

"The Neil boys still up there?"

He heard a rattle of newspaper and knew that the girl had again lowered it to look at him. He turned and saw her face. It was everything he'd imagined. Pretty enough to knock a man back on his heels. *To hell with the Neil boys,* he thought, *I wonder who she is*. He might have gone over, but she ducked behind the newspaper again.

The clerk was saying: "Sure, Oren and Bill Neil are still up there. Biggest outfit in the country now that the Learys went ka-flop and old man Dardis got killed. Young Mary Dardis, she's still milling, but she's down to one saw. Come to think of it, the Neil boys aren't up there exactly, either. They're right here in Red Bank. Came in yesterday. Staying right here at the hotel."

Leary, signing the register, had already seen their names.

He wrote his own name, and the clerk, reading it, said: "Leary! Say, *you* ain't one o' the Skidway Learys, are you? No relation to old Logger Leary that used to be the big *tyee* up there?"

"My dad."

The clerk whistled. He drew himself up and said: "In *that* case maybe we do have a room for you, after all. That'll be five dollars more."

"One seat in a crum show's as good as another. For five bucks I'll camp in the bullpen."

He wanted another look at the girl, but he didn't want to seem too anxious. Casually, with a swing of his long body, he turned, but she was gone. He barely glimpsed her leaving the front door. Outside, he had another brief view of her turning down a side street toward the railroad sheds.

He shrugged and dismissed her from his mind. He had a bath and a shave at a barbershop and, with the early darkness of northern November settling, found a stool in a steamy, crowded Chinese café. He'd just ordered a caribou steak when he realized that a man had come from somewhere and was standing behind him. He was a big man, very broad, with legs like a stud horse. Hatred went through Leary in a raw shock. The years had made him forget how he felt toward the man—Oren Neil.

Neil had run his father out of business. He'd done it cleverly, by maneuvering Leary and the Dardis Company into a timber war. Buzz Leary knew that now. He knew it, but the Neil boys didn't *know* that he knew it. Buzz had lifted the cup of coffee just placed in front of him. In the steamy, backbar mirror he saw Oren Neil's face. A smile turned the corners of Neil's mouth. He knew Buzz was watching him.

"Hello, Buzz," he said in a silky voice that was unexpected from a man of his rugged appearance. "So you came back to look up your old friends."

Leary went hot and cold. A clammy perspiration

sprang out along his hairline. He was thinking: *Here is the man who killed Steve Dardis, trampled him to death under his hobnailed boots.* It had been like this—Dardis had agreed to a night meeting with a Leary representative with a view to stopping the trouble that was bankrupting them. But in the morning, Dardis was found beaten to death, and the Leary representative had fled the country. Everyone blamed the Learys. The Learys even blamed themselves. "I should never have sent Hobs Donahue to talk with him," old Logger had said. But now Buzz knew the truth. Fighting to control his voice, he revolved on the stool and said: "Hello, Oren."

They shook hands. Neil asked pleasantly: "Still in the lumber business?"

He had a good look at Neil now. Five years hadn't changed him except to enlarge his jowls, but he wasn't fat. He was big and predatory, and, if one was to believe a large number of women, he was handsome. His frame was no larger than Leary's. He might have been an inch shorter, but he had a greater depth of muscle. Oren Neil used to brag that he'd never hired a timber jack he couldn't lick, and Leary knew it was true.

"Sure I'm in the lumber business," Leary said. "High rigger. Been working around Bella Colla."

"Heard you were on the Klondike."

"I was on Copper River."

"Back for good?"

"I'll be seeing how things look."

Oren Neil smiled, his narrow eyes showing he knew what was on Leary's mind. "The railroad changes things, doesn't it? It might even make that Caribou white pine of yours worth a piece of change. I dare say you could lumber it at a profit now." He scratched his jaw as though the idea had just occurred to him. "Yes, but it'd take capital. Twenty or thirty thousand dollars by the time you got your dad's old mill in shape."

There was no friendliness in Leary's voice when he said: "That's the thing of ours you wanted most and the thing you didn't get . . . the white pine."

"What are you talking about? It wasn't *us* that put your dad out of business, it was Dardis. If you came back here with a chip on your shoulder . . ."

"Don't play me for a fool, Oren. When those cheap lawyers were trying to buy that Caribou stand from me, I knew who was behind them."

Neil decided to laugh. "All right. So it was. How'd you find out?"

The truth was, Leary had thrust a lawyer three-fourths of the way from his sixth-story window in a Vancouver office building, threatening to drop him unless he got the truth. "I used persuasion."

"*I'll* use persuasion. Hold on, don't lose your temper. You're not a kid any longer. I think we'll get that Caribou pine when you find out you can make more by selling it to us than you can by trying to lumber it yourself."

"At six hundred a section?"

Neil laughed and said: "Oh, hell! Is that what he offered you? I don't wonder you used persuasion. You should have knocked his teeth down his throat. But this is no place to talk. Come back to the booth."

There were two small private rooms in the rear. In one of them was Oren's brother, Bill Neil, his elbows on the table, waiting. Bill was shorter than Oren, but heavier. His shoulders were massive, giving him a sloped gorilla appearance. He was unshaved. Tobacco stained the corners of his mouth and gave his black whiskers a rusty glint. He was dressed like a timber jack in a gray wool shirt, hobbed boots, a pair of tin pants so smeared with pitch and dirt they could have stood in the corner by themselves.

Bill grinned, leaned over to spit, and said: "Well, Buzz, so you're back in the old bush. And just when we was bragging about being shut of the Learys."

The greeting was one he'd have accepted cheerfully from even a casual acquaintance, but from Neil it was different. He felt anger burn through him and had a struggle to control himself. He said: "Us Learys keep coming back for more."

Bill stopped chewing and looked at him with narrowed little eyes. The kerosene lamp on its chain overhead brought out the brutal qualities of his face. Bill liked to effect a clumsy good nature, but the difference between the brothers was only superficial. At the bottom one was just as merciless as the other.

Bill said: "That's the idea! Keep coming back for more. Don't be a quitter. Trouble is, if you look around, you'll notice this country is near run out of Learys."

Oren hooked a chair with his boot toe and said: "That Gateway timber war burned itself out five years ago. Let's leave it that way. Here, kid, rest your hocks."

Leary pulled the chair around so the door was somewhat at his back, and sat down.

Oren said to Bill: "Leary and I have been talking about that Caribou pine. By the way, you know what that cheap lawyer offered him? . . . six hundred a section!" He laughed and struck the table with his hand. "I told him to buy as cheap as he could, *but six hundred!* I don't blame you for getting rough with him. What price do you have on it anyhow?"

"I don't think I want to sell."

Oren had been putting on a good act, but it froze now. Anger started to show in the thickening of his neck muscles, the rise of a vein at his temple. He'd been notorious for his temper, but now he was trying to keep hold of it.

"I'm sorry, Buzz. I thought you'd grown up. Got over being a hot-headed kid. Thought you were here on business. I have a legitimate proposition.

A *business* proposition. I'll pay you two thousand a section for that timber, and assume all unpaid liens and taxes. I'll grant that with the railroad going through you'd be able to timber it off yourself. If you were lucky, you'd make that much. But what's the use? I'm offering it to you without risk, all in the clear."

It was a good proposition. Leary knew that. He'd rather it hadn't been, so he'd have better reason for throwing it back in Oren's face.

"No, I don't think I'll sell to you." He didn't emphasize the "you" but that's the way Oren Neil took it.

"You mean you won't sell to the Neils?"

"That's right. I won't sell to the Neils."

Bill said: "What you got against us? We always tried to keep the peace in that Gateway country. It was your dad and Steve Dardis. They put themselves on the rocks."

"That's what I always thought." Leary felt the tightness that had settled. It was like the steel string of some instrument drawn tighter and tighter until it vibrates at the breaking point. The *clatter* of dishes seemed very loud out in the restaurant.

Bill said: "Now you're mad because Oren and me saved our money and bought in on Skidway after your dad went ka-flop. You . . ."

Oren said: "Keep still and let him say what he started to. Go ahead. What makes you think they didn't put themselves on the rocks?"

He hadn't intended to tell about meeting Hobs Donahue, but now all he wanted was to throw the truth in Oren Neil's face. He said: "My dad sent Hobs to make peace with Dardis. He shouldn't have sent him alone. He should have known somebody might be waiting for him on the trail."

Oren Neil was pale around the mouth while his neck was gorged with blood. If Buzz had any doubt that Hobs Donahue had been telling the truth, that doubt was gone now. Usually Oren was the dominant one of the two, but at that moment it was Bill who could laugh and dribble tobacco juice at the floor.

"Now who'd be waiting for Hobs?" Bill asked. "You're letting your suspicions run away with you, putting one and one together and coming up with a double dozen. Use your head, Buzz. You know as well as anybody that Hobs hated Steve Dardis's guts."

"I should have told you in the first place. I ran Hobs down in the city. The two of you and Claggett killed Dardis."

Oren Neil was halfway out of his chair, his legs bent, hands poised. He seemed ready to spring. He spoke through tense lips: "You believe what you want to. I ran your drunken father out of business, I'll own up to that. I hope you turn my offer down. I hope you try to log the Caribou yourself. I hope so, because I'll run you out of the country, too."

Leary stood half turned away. He looked casual and limber-armed compared with Oren Neil. Then he moved and swung a savage right hand to the point of Oren's jaw. It smashed Oren back. He half fell over the chair. His shoulders struck the wall so hard one of the panels ripped loose. He bounced back, grabbed the table with his left hand, and upset it, trying to pin Leary against the wall.

Leary had the door back of him. He kicked it open and stopped just outside, knowing that now both men couldn't come for him at once. Bill Neil was struggling over the table. Oren shoved him aside and was through the door. He came with a bull charge, his hands flung far ahead. Leary retreated another step, set his feet, and brought up a one-two left and right. Oren caught part of their power with his arms. They didn't break his momentum. He was heavier than Leary, and, in the crowded quarters between the wall and the row of stools in front of the counter, it was his advantage. He carried Leary before him as men bellowed and climbed out of the way.

Leary hit the wall with his right hip. He did it deliberately as sometimes he'd used the boards in a hockey rink. It made him pivot sharply, roll with the charge. It placed him with his back to the wall and Oren Neil close in front of him. He planted his right foot on the wall, feinted high with a left, and brought up a right that snapped Oren's head to one side and dropped him to the floor. He lit in a sitting position, between two of the stools, his shoulders against the counter. For just a second his eyes lacked focus. He lunged to his feet. The force of his doing it rocked the entire length of counter and sent a crash of dishes to the floor. Buzz was on him, slugging with both hands, and Oren, still a little groggy, fought him off, retreating through the door to the corduroy log walk outside.

Oren rolled with a left and came back with a barrage that made Leary give ground. The logs gave an uncertain footing. Something struck him on the back of the leg. He tried to step over it. It tripped him. As he fell, he saw Bill Neil crouched low to the walk with one leg thrust out. Leary tried to twist over and save himself, but Oren Neil saw his chance and was atop him with the speed and ferocity of a great cat. He swung a heavy, hobnailed boot, and it struck like an explosion inside Leary's brain.

He was down. Fragments of consciousness were like voices screaming in his ear, telling him to crawl away, to keep his arms wrapped around his head, but the boots struck again and again as he felt the diminishing shock of them.

He came to by slow degrees. It seemed like hours. There were voices, a man and a woman. Finally he realized that they had him on his feet and were walking him somewhere. He felt slush underfoot. He was going across a street. He was aware of lights then, and his head commenced paining with repeated stabs, as though a knife was working back and forth, cutting his brain in half. He was thirsty. He tried to say something. His lips seemed thick. All his teeth ached. Neil had really given him the hobs. The crowd looking on had probably saved his life. Otherwise, he'd have got it the same way Steve Dardis had.

A girl had hold of one of his arms. He turned and looked at her. Through puffed eyes he could tell she was small, and dark-haired, with a lovely, thin face. Even smashed up as he was it seemed strange to him that such a girl would be here, beside him, wading the muck of this tough construction town.

A big Finlander had hold of his other arm. "You got room in ho-tal, kid?"

Leary grinned and managed to say: "Sure, up in the bullpen."

"I have a room," the girl said.

Men sat beneath the hanging lamps in the tiny lobby, staring at them as they walked through, and down a hall to a door with a brass number 8 nailed on it. She opened it with a skeleton key and said to the Finlander: "I'll take care of him now."

He backed away, fumbling with his cap, and she closed the door. It was dark for a moment inside the room, and Leary heard her moving around. Then she struck a match, lit the lamp, adjusted the wick. The underlighting did something to her face. It gave her skin a tawny appearance, brought out the softness of her throat, accentuated her thin nostrils, the delicate, wedge-like shape of her face. Her eyes were dark, but the hair he first took to be black had a rich coppery sheen with the lamplight striking close against it. She turned, and he was aware of the full lines of her body. She smiled at him, and took off her jacket.

"You'd better sit down," she said.

Her voice sounded different now. Soft and rather husky. He sank down in a straight-backed chair, still looking at the woman. She wore a dress of some soft, woolly material. Wine red. It wasn't tight, it was just cut to fit, and the material hung to the curves of her young body. She was fragile and feminine. It was the way a woman ought to look. A woman who is not ashamed of being a woman. The dress had broad straps over the shoulders, and beneath it she had on a blouse of white silk, open at the throat.

She found a towel, dipped it in the water pitcher, and squeezed it out. "You're cut awfully. Maybe I should get a doctor."

"You'll do." He tried to grin.

She came around behind him and started rubbing the towel gently over his face. Seated, he was almost as tall as she was. He was aware of her closeness, of the subtle perfume she wore. He looked around the room. Her suitcase was open on the floor. She'd hung a couple of dresses on wire hangers behind a rusty-looking curtain that served as a closet. The bed had been slept in. There were no sheets on it. Gray, cotton blankets still bearing the impression of her body. She hadn't disturbed much more of the bed than a kitten. It occurred to him that she must have slept through the day and just got up.

"Does it hurt?" she asked.

He moved like a man waking up and said: "Just a little."

"What were you fighting about?"

The battle seemed far away, a nightmare scene, another world.

"We're old . . . friends. Did you see it?"

"Yes." She whispered the word so intensely that he turned to look at her. Her eyes were bright, and she was biting down hard on her underlip. "Yes, I saw it. It frightened me, but I couldn't stop looking. Even when you were down and he was stamping on you . . . I thought he was killing you, but still I had to watch. Every second of it."

"Ever see men fight before?"

She shook her head.

"You'll see it every night in this town. What are you doing here, anyway?"

"Why should you ask?" There was defiance and bitterness in her voice. "Isn't it enough that I get a man to help me drag you in off the street and . . . ?"

"Yes, that's enough. It just didn't seem to me

you ought to be here. In a town like Red Bank."

She whispered: "I'm a dance-hall girl. Didn't you notice? I'm wearing a red dress."

"You're not a dance-hall girl!" he said with sudden violence.

She stopped rubbing him with the towel. It was bloody from his face and scalp. She dipped it in the pitcher and squeezed it out, her eyes on the pinkish water that boiled around her white and slender fingers.

"You're just a boy, really."

"I'm not a boy, and you're not a dance-hall girl."

She spoke in a voice that sounded a trifle tired: "I came here to sing in a music hall. I guess there's a difference." She was before him again, bathing his face. Her hands were warm and soft. She said: "You didn't want me to be a dance-hall girl?"

"No." He reached for her.

She stopped and let her elbows press down hard across his neck, against his chest. He felt her body against him for a few seconds, and she whispered: "I'm glad."

He got out of the chair. In doing it, his knees turned and almost failed him after serving him through all the battle.

She backed away and shook her head. "Please. I shouldn't have done that. It's just that you're such a nice fellow. Don't get any ideas. Sit down and let me finish cleaning you up."

He took the towel from her and rubbed hard to get the rest of the blood off his face. Then he looked at himself in the rusty mirror. Oren Neil's hobs had cut deep furrows in both cheeks that were still oozing blood. Both his eyes were blackened; his lips were puffed; his face was swollen on one side more than the other. He felt better now, however. Only a slight headache.

He fished tobacco and papers from his shirt pocket and, while rolling one, said: "I'll live. I'll live and give Oren and Bill both another chance at me. I hope the hell it'll be one at a time, though."

She opened a gold mesh bag and took out a packet of cigarettes. "Have one of these." And she added: "I always carry them for my father."

"Where is he?"

She laughed and said: "Last I heard of him, he was dealing faro down in the States." She puffed a cigarette to light over the lamp, put it between his mashed lips, and lighted one for herself. "You don't mind seeing me smoke? After all, this is Nineteen Oh Eight. The era of women's rights." Her lapel watch was ticking on the dresser. The hands stood at eight o'clock. "I haven't eaten since yesterday."

"Why, girl . . . ?"

"Last night at Trout Creek. I came in on the train this afternoon."

He looked at her sharply. He'd been through

both passenger cars. They'd been filled with construction workers recruited in towns eastward along the line. Two women, but neither had been she.

Her eyes narrowed, and for an instant she reminded him of a cornered animal, then she smiled, showing the tips of her teeth and said: "You look like you doubted me."

"I came in on it is all. I didn't notice you."

"But I was there. No, I'm not escaping from the law. But let's not talk about it. You'd hate me if you knew the truth. That's why I wouldn't let you put your arms around me a minute ago. I'm not good enough for a kid like you."

Kid! It sounded funny. She wasn't as old as he was. He started to say so, and she cut him off.

"I'm hungry. Have you forgotten?"

"There's that chink dump. . . ."

"No. Not there. The variety theater. There's some private booths upstairs. The owner, Klondike Williams, I know him well."

# II

Klondike Williams was a quick-moving man of fifty with a cockney accent. He spoke to the girl, calling her—"Etty."—and gave Buzz Leary a sharp, rat-like glance.

"Sing tonight?" Klondike asked.

"No, we're just hungry." She tucked her hand under Leary's arm while Klondike grinned, showing a row of gold-tipped teeth. "How about one of the cubbyholes upstairs?"

"Ow, listen to 'er! Class, w'at?" He shook his head. "Not a chance. We got the gold-plated bunch in 'em tonight, we 'ave for a certainty. Maxwell Phare, travelin' super no less for Dominion Limited. And in the other, Mister Oren Neil *and* a lady friend."

The words, Leary decided, were aimed at him and he made a start as though to grab the man, but Etty got in front of him.

She said to Klondike: "How much you got tied up in those gold choppers?"

"Too much to want 'em knocked out, m'sweet. Now that's a fact. For you and the gentleman . . . a box with a view of the stage. Best in the 'ouse." He gave Leary another sharp look. "It's cash, ain't it?"

"It's cash."

The box was a tiny cubicle with a table and two slim, gilded chairs. A decorated screen covered the front of it, hiding them, but allowing a view of the stage and the floor below. The show hadn't started, but there was music from a violin, clarinet, and harp. In a few minutes a Chinese boy entered in soft-slippered silence and placed on the table a bottle of champagne and a large bowl of iced oysters on the half shell.

"I didn't know we'd ordered," Leary said while his puffed, hob-scraped face made him look mean.

Etty gave him a reproachful pout and said: "They expect you to have this when you take a box."

"I don't want to go second-class. I just want to order."

"You likee beef steak?" the Chinese boy asked, smiling. "You likee rare?"

"I could use a raw one for my face."

He tore off the sealing wire on the champagne bottle, and sprung the cork so it popped and left a tiny froth mark on the ceiling. He did it with a deftness that showed he'd opened such bottles before and Etty clapped her hands with the delight of a small child. He filled the glasses, drank, and commenced wolfing the oysters. Hungry, the first drink hit him hard. There was more food, a great deal of talk, and the show going on. She kept filling his glass. Without his noticing it, the place had filled up. The floor below was now a solid mass of rough-clad, rough-talking men, a few frilly-dressed women, all swimming beneath a haze of bluish tobacco smoke. The bottle was empty. Afterward he had only a fuzzy recollection of popping a second cork. Wine, tobacco smoke, noise, and music, the closeness of the girl—all of it seemed mixed up together.

It was a warm current carrying him ever deeper and deeper, then suddenly he knew he was getting drunk, and with an effort he brought himself to concentrate on his surroundings. He was like a drowning man who finds it's easier to come up than it is to stay at the surface. His head buzzed; his eyes came to focus on the table. He realized they'd finished one bottle of champagne and were halfway through a second; the table bore the remains of steak, and baked potato, and Russian fish eggs. He'd always disliked fish eggs and the people who ate them. He'd been there a long time. It must have been midnight. Down on the stage two men in loud suits, straw hats, and bamboo canes were hoofing and singing in brassy unison:

Way down on the o-old plantation
I had eight women makin' love to me;
Now Monday it was Linda's turn,
And Tuesday it was Jane's,
And Wednesday I was merry as could be-e. . . .

He noticed Etty watching him. She had a cigarette in one corner of her mouth. Smoke curled past her face.

He said: "Let's get out of this dive."

"Sure, if you want to." But she didn't move. She seemed to be waiting for him, wanting him to come to her.

He stood and took a single step around the little table. He seized her beneath her arms, lifted her. She remained perfectly passive, her head tilted back, her eyes almost closed. He kissed her, drew her hard against him, and kissed her again. Her lips were soft and slightly wet from champagne.

He came to with the sun shining through the dirty windows of a big room. He'd been sleeping in his soogins on the floor. He sat up. His face was still puffed and stiff-feeling from Oren Neil's hobs. Inside, he was worse. He spat and shook his head. Finally he brought his aching eyes to focus on the details of the room. It was square and bare with benches around two sides. Here and there were bedrolls, but no one was in sight. He saw a washstand and a big brass pitcher. The pitcher was empty. He cursed and hurled it at the door. It struck with a *clang* that was like a pain in his ears. He heard a man running along the hall. The door opened. It was the old white-haired clerk.

"What the hell!" He picked up the pitcher and tried to decide which of its dents was new. "Say, you been out on a dandy!"

"Fill it up."

He did. Buzz Leary stood over the basin, naked to the waist, while he poured it over him. The cold water felt good.

"Face full o' hobs and a gut full o' champagne all in one night. By damn, you Learys can really take it."

"I feel like I took it, all right."

He threw open the window and stood in the

cold November draft until he was dry.

"You'll get pneumonia," the clerk said.

"That'd be an improvement."

"You don't hold your likker very good, kid."

He always had in the past. Last night it had hit him between the eyes. That first drink. He'd been sitting there, dipping oysters in tomato sauce, and wham-o! "Proves an Irishman should stick with straight whiskey."

The old man said: "One time I had a pal that got rolled in a plush house over at Kitnik. That's a salmon town out on the coast. Gal knocked some cigarette ash in his drink. You counted your money this morning, kid?"

"If you think that girl lifted my roll . . ."

"I don't think nothing. I ain't saying nothing against her, either. That big grizzly, Oren Neil, would just as soon knock my head off like he did yours."

"What's he got to do with it?"

"I don't know that, either." He looked around quickly. "I wish I hadn't brought it up. Don't ring me in on it, y'hear? But I'll tell you this. Some of the boys say he was in a fancy café with her down in Vancouver a couple months ago. Then she shows up here."

"Sure she's the same one?"

"How could I be sure? All I know is what some of the boys say. Figure she followed him here. Women have a hankering for him."

Leary looked at the door after the old man was gone. He walked over and found his pants, located his wallet, opened it. He'd hit town with $55 in currency and about $200 in gold. Currency still there—all but $60 of the gold. He hadn't been rolled. In fact, he'd come out of it rather well. Champagne and caviar!

At the railroad office Leary learned that a barge would leave for Skidway next morning at sunup. He had no difficulty securing passage, put the rubber-stamped EMPLOYEE slip in his shirt pocket, and went back to the hotel. It was mid-afternoon then, and Etty was waiting for him. He'd been suspicious of her, but it all vanished when he saw her—small, smooth, and so pretty. He knew he hadn't been drugged, and he decided to ask bluntly about Oren Neil.

"Neil?" she said. "Oh, the man you were fighting with. No, I don't know him. Why?"

"Someone said you were with him in Vancouver a couple of months ago. Said you followed him here."

"That's silly. I haven't been in Vancouver for over a year. I never saw Oren Neil before last night. Not that I know of, anyway." She reached up and brushed her fingers gently on his left cheek. "Does that hurt? The cuts have all turned purple."

"I'm not a very good sight, am I?"

"I think you're a very good sight. How do you

feel? I've had a headache all day. I'm not much of a party girl. I haven't had anything to eat. Do you suppose dinner would help me?"

He took her to the Paradise. The place was dim and quiet now. It had been cleaned out, but there was still a stale smell of tobacco. A few men were at the bar and card games. This time they went to one of the private dining rooms she'd asked about last night. The same Chinese boy came in with a tray, put whiskey, glasses, and bottled fizz water on the table.

Etty mixed herself a whiskey and fizz, but Leary merely poured himself straight fizz. "Henry Ward Beecher style," he said.

She pouted. "I won't drink mine then." She was like a sulky kitten. "I shouldn't have brought you here. I thought . . ."

"Oh, hell!" He laughed, filled the glass the rest of the way with whiskey. "There, if it'll make you feel better."

"It will make you feel better. Really, it will."

It did. It took the residue of ache from his head, wiped the resin taste off his tongue. Food was a long time coming. He had a couple more drinks. Suddenly he realized the liquor was hitting him again. He stood and said: "I need some fresh air."

She got up, small and quiet, and walked to the door. Her jacket was tossed over a chair. He thought she was going outside in just her thin, wool dress. She didn't open the door, though. She put her hands behind her, leaned her shoulders against it, and stood looking up at him.

"I love you, you know." Her words were frank and they jolted him to a stop. She was breathing rapidly. She seemed excited. He started to say something but she shook her head. "You're not the first man I've said that to. I swore I'd *never* say it to a man again. But now I have."

"Etty!" he said, and took hold of her arms just below the shoulders. She moved back and forth, trying to pull away, but the door was against her shoulders. "Etty, tell me about yourself. What are you running away from?"

"You want to know? Buzz, let me go. I'll show you. You can *see,* then you'll know what I'm running away from."

He let loose of her. She reached back over her shoulders. She was unbuttoning her dress. She drew it down and held it across her bosom with both hands while revealing the skin of her shoulders. Criss-crossing them were welt marks several months old.

"He whipped me. My husband. Now you know. He was no good, Buzz. He couldn't even hold a job. I sang and he drank up the money. Then he imagined things about me with other men and whipped me. He took his belt off and whipped me."

"You poor kid! That's why you ran away?"

Again, as the night before, she was in his arms. She sobbed and clung tightly to him, her cheek pressed against his flannel shirt. She clung tighter and tighter as though he was the last thing she had and all else was a howling wilderness.

"Yes, I ran away. But he'll follow me. He'll find me. I have to sing in these places to earn a living. Somebody he knows will be sure to see me and let him know where I am."

"Where is this fellow?"

She shook her head. "Don't let him come and take me."

"I'll break his neck if he comes around."

"Take me away from here, Buzz." She let go the front of his shirt and tossed her arms around his neck. "Oh, Buzz, take me away. Take me where I'll never hear of him again. Take me away!"

"You don't have to run away from him. If he comes around . . ."

"Oh, Buzz, I'm a foolish girl. I've never seen anything. Take me with you. Show me those places you've been. The cities, Montreal. Please, Buzz, take me to Montreal."

"On six hundred and eighty dollars?"

"I have a couple hundred."

"That's not enough. Etty, listen to me . . ."

"But we can get by. You can play hockey. You must have some way of raising a few thousand. You're a Leary! You're from a great lumbering family."

"Let's talk about it tomorrow."

She flung herself in a chair, bent over, and cried with her head in her hands. "I was a fool. Of course you don't love me."

He tried to comfort her. She asked him to have another drink with her. She poured it. It was a tremendous slug.

"Now, listen, Etty . . ."

A long time later he'd half promised to sell out and take her away with him. The orchestra was playing, and somehow or other they got back in one of the theater boxes. A voice inside Leary's brain kept saying: *You can't keep this up night after night.* It was a box on the lower tier this time, but strangely those same brassy comedians were on stage, hoofing and singing:

> Way down on the o-old plantation
> I had eight women makin' love to me. . . .

Leary said good night to the girl and went inside the bullpen where ten or twelve men were snoring in their soogins on the floor. It was just commencing to get light outside. Clear and raw, with a gusty wind from the northwest. An engine down on the tracks kept switching around and tooting its whistle. It would be good, he was thinking, to take her to Montreal. The thought of taking her there made him sick and gutless. And the money was easy to get. Just sell that Caribou timber.

He didn't dare see her again. He didn't dare go to bed, miss the barge. He wasn't man enough to say no to her. He'd always had contempt for men who could be wrapped around a woman's finger. He groped across the room, found his soogins, rolled them up with his extra clothes, and went outside.

The wind struck him; it felt good to him, good and clean with a sharpness to it that carried away the fumes of whiskey, tobacco, and perfume. He walked to the railroad yards and among the vast, sprawling warehouses to the river docks where 100 or more men were at work with handcarts and horse carts, hauling construction equipment down and loading it on big square-ended barges. These would run the current downstream and unload at camps here and there along Gateway Cañon where excavation and grading crews were at work, preparing the roadbed in advance of the rails.

He asked the loading boss about the Skidway barge. It was pointed out to him—a roofed-over boat with its own steam engine. In another hour it was sunup, and he stood on the barge deck, watching Red Bank as it grew small and was engulfed by forest. For a distance of twelve miles the railroad lay along the north bank, then it ended, and they kept passing construction camps, each with its stretch of partly finished grade. Late that afternoon, after passing the last of the construction camps, the barge cleared a point and the town of Skidway was in view.

Buzz Leary stood with his elbows on the rail, a cigarette between his still-swollen lips, looking at it. Things had changed. When he was a boy, there'd been seven sawmills operating within a ten-mile radius. Now there were no more than a couple. The barge, swinging close to shore, gave him a brief view of his father's old mill. The big building was vacant and weather-browned brush had sprung up around it.

The docks of the town were a half mile farther. He got off, hoisted his war sack on his shoulder, and walked up the corduroyed walks. Most of the town was old and drab, but here and there a new building was going up in anticipation of the day the division headquarters were moved here from Red Bank. There were lots of men on the streets, a few timber jacks and mill hands, but most of them were with the railroad engineering crew. He walked along the length of Main Street before he saw a man he knew. It was the barber, Jake Culliton.

He shook hands with Jake and asked about his old friends. Most of them were gone, following the timber north and west. Big Torg was still here, however. That was Torg Torgerson, his father's old mill boss. He was operating a little tie mill of his own back in Comas Gulch.

It was deep winter twilight when Leary got

there. Torg, a huge, blunt man, plodded down, peering at him. It took him a few seconds to realize who it was, then he almost cried. They had supper together—Leary, Torg, and his three big-framed sons.

"Ay always know those damn' Neil boys bane at the bottom of it," Big Torg said when Leary told him about his visit with Hobs.

In the morning Leary and Torg went down to inspect the abandoned sawmill. Most of the equipment was still there, but it would take $15,000 to put it in shape. Then, with the shadow of evening settling in the timber, he walked northward from town up a narrow-gauge logging railroad toward the north mill of the Enterprise Company that Mary Dardis had somehow managed to salvage from the wreckage left by the Dardis-Leary timber war.

Big Torg had warned him: "You bane fool to go up there. By golly, that girl, she's tougher than man. Shoot gun like man. Long time ago she lose that mill, only nobody have guts to go up there and serve bank paper. Her log boss, he's tough, too. Name's Franzen. You look out for him."

The tracks took him up a wide gulch through timber. It had snowed a little since the last train of cars had been down. The tracks, he could see, were in a fair state of repair. After half an hour of steady walking a sign beside the tracks stopped him. TRESPASSING FORBIDDEN, and in small letters: VISITORS PLEASE WAIT FOR WATCHMAN.

He stood for a while, but it was growing late, and he decided to walk on. The repeated *screech* of a gang saw came to his ears; on the air was the sour, pitchy odors of a mill. He kept thinking of Mary Dardis as he walked. She'd been a quiet, scrawny, freckled kid when he last saw her. He couldn't imagine her getting very rough—didn't seem like the same girl Big Torg had described. He was wondering what he'd say to her when a gunshot broke his reverie. A bullet scorched the back of his neck, and the next moment he realized he was on his stomach, scrambling down the railroad ditch.

He felt his neck and looked for blood. There wasn't any. The bullet had missed, but it hadn't been aimed to miss. It had been aimed to kill. He lay in a foot of snow in the railroad ditch, safe only for a moment. He raised himself on hands and knees, took a quick glance around. His only escape was on up the hillside. He sprang, made it in three long strides. The gun *cracked* again. Its high-velocity slug tore rocks and dirt from under the snow and stung his legs. He lunged through a tangle of fox brush as a third bullet *whanged* past.

He paused on one knee and looked around. While running, he'd glimpsed the gun flash. It was eighty or ninety yards away, at the shadowy crest of a bank. Whoever it was wouldn't stay there. He'd move and try to cut him off. He'd naturally expect that Leary would turn back toward town. That's where he was wrong. He'd come up there to talk with Mary Dardis.

He grinned as he rubbed his taped-up knee and thought that maybe she was the one shooting at him. Darkness was settling, and that was in his favor. He moved uphill slowly, followed a deer trail across rock and fallen timber. He glimpsed lights through the trees. It was the mill. He sat on his heels, rolled a cigarette, and puffed it cold while looking down on the mill. He'd seen it eight or ten years before when the Enterprise Company was one of the big ones in that part of British Columbia. Now it was only partly kept up, perhaps operating at a scant one-third capacity. Below him were some bunkhouses with tar-papered roofs, a wanigan house, some sheds. The saw kept *screeching* intermittently, and in moments of silence he could hear a man playing an accordion and singing in Swedish. The mill office was farther off, and up a low hillside. That's where he'd be most likely to find her.

He made a circle of the mill, came to the building by a rear path, listened at the door. No lights or sound, but a wisp of wood smoke was rising from the stovepipe. He rapped, and, getting no answer, he went inside, groped through a length of hall, and reached the big room that was a combination living room and office. He could see the general outlines of it by the slight glow that came from the open draft of the stove. "Hello!" he said, thinking someone might be asleep in one of the wall bunks, then he went on, found a chair beside the stove, and sat down. The unlighted cigarette had all the while been between his lips. He bit off the sodden end, opened the stove door, lighted up, then he settled back to wait for someone to come in.

He finished the cigarette and another. A loose board *thudded* out front, warning of someone's approach. He heard voices, the door opened, and a girl came in. She stopped, and was looking around. It was too dark for her to see him, but the air was filled with the smell of a cigarette. Her hand had moved back, the fingers long and slim, pointed downward, just touching the butt of her revolver. Her posture reminded him of a startled animal. She had that kind of grace, the grace of a panther. That was the impression he had, seeing her just inside the door, faintly revealed against the light of a rising moon. He'd been prepared for her—for Mary Dardis. *This couldn't be Mary Dardis,* he was thinking. She'd been scrawny and bony and skinny-legged. This girl was none of those things.

He said: "Don't draw that gun. I've had enough people shoot at me for one day."

"Who are you?" Her voice was high-pitched. It showed the tremble of nervousness inside her. It was like the vibration of a string drawn too tightly.

He said: "Now, just stand there, and I'll show you." He wanted to give her time to steady herself. She was on the point of whipping that gun from its holster, and, unless appearances went for nothing, she'd be a wildcat once she cut loose. He leaned over, opened the stove door, threw his cigarette inside. She saw his face then, strongly lighted by the fire, but it was apparent she didn't recognize him.

She said: "Well?"

"I'm Buzz Leary."

The words hit her. She moved instinctively, a light-footed, cat-like pivot, and the gun came from the holster. She checked herself with it rocked back in the heel of her palm, ready to fire.

He cried: "Use your head, girl!" He saw her stop, her legs spread. She wore trousers, regular tin pants, but on her they were different. Even scared for his life, he couldn't help admiring the way her legs molded into them. "You wouldn't want to shoot me. Not on this nice, clean floor."

She let the pistol barrel tilt toward the floor. Her eyes were still intense and a little wild, but he guessed he was safe enough. As safe as a man ever is with a redhead.

She said: "Light the lamp!"

He scratched a match. The lamp was on a chain above. He stood on a chair, lighted it, adjusted the wick. While he was doing it, he had a good look at her. She was medium in height, with hair the color of liquid copper. Her eyes were intensely blue. The tin pants, held up by a belt, were cinched tightly around her waist. She was slim anyway, and the belt made her look slimmer. What she would have been in one of Etty's dresses! She wore small logger boots, a Mackinaw, a man's hat. She was Mary Dardis, though. She still had the freckles across the bridge of her nose, and there was that old mannerism—her way of tilting her head to one side when she looked at him.

He said: "Well, Mary, this is a funny way to meet an old friend."

Her little chin was jutted out, her lips were tight. "Did you think I'd forgotten? Did you think I could ever forget that the Learys killed my father?"

He said earnestly: "We didn't kill him, Mary."

"If that's all you came here to say . . ."

"It's not. I came here to tell you the whole story."

"Well, I'm not going to listen." Her hand was very tight around the gun. Her finger, clenched on the trigger, had started the hammer back on its double-action mechanism. Her lips were pulled back. He could see her perfect white teeth. She spoke through them: "I know what you Learys are. I know what *you* are. You came back from the city and now you think you can make a simple backwoods girl listen to your lies."

"You're afraid of me, aren't you?"

She reacted as though to a slap in the face. He thought for a second that he'd gone too far, that this time she would fire. Her breast, swelling the Mackinaw, rose and fell rapidly. She said: "Afraid of you?" She laughed and jerked her head backwards, swinging the coils of coppery hair that fell from beneath her hat. "You haven't noticed, but I've got the gun."

He got another cigarette going and laughed at her with it scissored in one side of his mouth. "Sure, you're afraid. You're afraid of having to admit the truth. It'd make you feel like a fool, damning the Learys all these years, and trying to kill me on my way up here this evening. Sure you're afraid of me. You're afraid of listening to me."

She hissed: "Get out."

"No, not till I talk. Go ahead and pull the trigger. That's the only way you can stop me. Sure, I was down in the city. I was in Vancouver, blowing in my summer's wages. I never was any good, you know. Well, somebody broke a table over my head and I woke up in the hospital. You know who I found there, in one of the other wards? Hobs Donahue. He was dying. He told me about that night he went to meet your father. My dad sent him to make peace, but when Hobs got to the woods trail where your father was to meet him, the Neil boys and Claggett were ahead of him.

"They offered him five hundred dollars if he'd

tell your father to go to the devil. When Hobs wouldn't do it, they slugged him and tied him up. Then your father came, and they jumped him. Maybe they didn't intend to kill him. Not at first. Just beat him up, knowing us Learys would get the blame for it. But your father saw who it was, so all they could do was finish him off. Hobs knew he'd be blamed and end with a rope around his neck, so he got out of the country."

Her lips were closed, slanted down at the corners. She didn't believe him. "More Leary lies!"

"Look around and see who the winners were in that timber fracas if you think it's a lie."

A man had come through the door and was in the shadow, watching them. Leary could tell little about him, except that he was tall, and that he stood with the hunched manner affected by many tall men who wish to minimize their height. The man said in a slightly nasal tone: "You want me to take care of him, Miss Dardis?"

Leary said: "Is that your bushwhack specialist, Mary?"

"What were you talking about . . . somebody trying to kill you on your way here? If you have some sort of lie cooked . . ."

"It's no lie. Somebody shot at me. I was coming up the railroad."

"Our watchman has orders to keep everybody off. If you walked through our sign, maybe he decided to throw a scare into you."

"Scorch the back of a man's neck at ninety yards . . . some scare!"

The man walked forward then, into the light. He was in his late thirties, very skinny, with a narrow face, a high-ridged nose, and eyes that pressed closely against it. A lever-action Winchester hung in the crook of his arm.

"He's lying," he said to Mary, but Leary could hear him. "I shot, all right. Shot three times to put him on the run, but there wasn't a bullet came within twenty feet of him."

Leary said: "You must be Franzen."

His eyes showed a slight twitch of surprise. "Yah."

Big Torg had mentioned him, said he was tough. Torg had been right about everything. With Franzen backing her, Mary Dardis rammed her revolver back into its holster. Her Mackinaw was unbuttoned, but the room was still too hot with the fire going, so she took it off. She looked better the more he saw of her. She threw her hat aside, too, shook out her thick mass of hair, forked it back with her fingers. He knew that she was tired from doing a man's work, but pride wouldn't let her show it.

She said: "What are you doing back here? And let's have the truth this time."

"I haven't had much luck with the truth so far. Always heard you couldn't reason with a red-head." She stood with her hands on her hips, her head up. She was so pretty he forgot for a moment what he was talking about. "You know, I still own that stand of white pine up in the Sag. It'll be worth a quarter million when the rails go through. No good to me, though. I haven't got a mill. I notice you have one here and nothing much except silvery hemlock to feed it. It's a chance for both of us."

"No. I may go broke, but I'll not go in partnership with a Leary!"

# III

In the morning, Leary went downriver to the temporary rail camp at Big Bend. There the railroad survey turned from the river and headed eastward through the Kenaba Sag. The Sag was hilly and dissected by deep gulches, but it afforded no major obstacle to the railroad as did the mountain ranges north and south. A wagon road had been built by the engineering crew and he caught a ride as far as Caribou Creek, camping there, alone, beneath the shadow and silence of the big pines.

It had never been timbered. The Sag had no stream large enough to float such logs. He cruised the timber, blocked it out to decide which section could be timbered with the least cost. Returning, he stopped briefly at Skidway, hired a steam launch to Red Bank, and took the supply train on to Trout Creek. There he saw Dwight Gordon, one of Dominion Limited's vice presidents, and made a deal to sell one tenth of the entire Caribou stand in the form of saw logs that the railroad would saw at its own mill at Vermilion Lake. At Gordon's insistence he signed a guarantee to deliver by June 1st 4,000,000 board feet to a siding that the railroad would build up Long Tom Gulch. On the strength of that he received an advance payment, half of which he immediately spent on yarding equipment. When he got back to Skidway, a blizzard was on, and the engineering crew had laid off eighteen men who he immediately hired and put to work, twelve of them at the Caribou constructing winter camp under the direction of Big Torg and two of his boys, the rest at the old Skidway mill.

He lacked capital to reopen the mill, but no one except himself and the railroad front office knew of the deal he had, and he wanted the Neils to assume he planned on sawing the Caribou pine himself. They wouldn't sit back and let him make a profit on the very stand that had been their greatest ambition for twelve years. They'd try to stop him but, not knowing his deal with Gordon, maybe they'd try at the wrong place.

For three weeks things went along without a hitch. He spent most of his time at Caribou where the shacks were up and the crew had progressed to the point of building rollways. It was late

December then, with the strong cold setting in. Late one night he came down from Caribou and approached the mill to hear the high, insistent barking of Babine, a malamute belonging to Ole Torgerson.

Ole generally kept the animal inside a large wire pen back of the bunkhouse, but tonight he'd got loose. Leary followed the sound through an area of second-growth spruce. He heard a man then, cursing through his teeth, apparently trying to fight the dog away. A gun exploded, and instantly the dog was silent. The bullet must have struck him in the brain.

Leary ran. He took long strides, following the twisted path through the timber, and suddenly the man was right ahead of him. His back was turned. He started to run. They collided. The man fell away, trying to twist as he did so and bring his revolver up, but Leary fell with him, twisting his arm to make the gun fall. He knew who it was. Franzen—that tall log boss of Mary Dardis's. He'd had something in his left hand. A can. The gassy odor of kerosene was on the air. Leary did not pause. He rolled, still gripping Franzen's wrist, came to a crouch, pivoted, and had him in a whip lock with which he could twist his arm off at the shoulder. Franzen screamed from pain and Leary stopped. He placed a foot beneath Franzen's armpit and jerked the arm little by little, watching his face contort from pain.

"Who sent you to burn me out?"

Franzen panted and whimpered at the end of each breath. "Mary. She said . . . she'd burn you . . . run you out of the country."

It was what Leary both expected and hated to hear. He'd come there to fight the Neils, not Mary Dardis. He let him go. He stood over him for a few seconds. When he got up, Leary hit him with the heel of his palm and knocked him down again.

"Who was it sent you?"

"I hope to die it was Mary. She told me to shoot to kill that night at the north mill, too. What the hell do you want me to do? Lie and say it was Oren Neil?"

The kerosene can he'd been carrying was heavy metal. It had overturned and was leaking slowly. Franzen bent to pick it up. As he stopped, he whirled and swung it at Leary's head. Leary knew it would be coming. He weaved away and beneath it. As it whisked over him, he stepped in and smashed a right to Franzen's jaw. Franzen went down on his back. He lit hard and bounced on the pathway. He was out cold with blood running from the corners of his open mouth. Leary picked him up, got him over his shoulder, carried him up to the road. By that time, Ole Torgerson was coming to see what the trouble was. Leary told him to hitch the team. He was going to the north mill.

Franzen came to and sat up in the box of the

sled. His jaw had been broken in a couple of places, and he was hunched over, holding it with both hands all the way past town and up the gulch. No one challenged them. Leary pulled in as close as he could get to the mill office and shouted Mary's name until she came to the door with a quilt wrapped around her.

"Here he is, kerosene and all!"

Franzen got to his feet, but he didn't offer to help himself from the sled, so Leary gave him the shoulder, knocking him off the back. He sat in the snow, still holding his jaw. Leary threw the can of kerosene out beside him. Mary shouted some-thing, but he didn't wait. He drove downhill at a stiff trot, his winter collar up, muffling whatever she called after him.

When he got back, he learned from Ole that a girl had been there the previous afternoon looking for him. He asked who she was, and had that gutless feeling at the same time knowing it would be Etty. She'd followed him from Red Bank.

"What's she doing in Skidway?" he asked.

"Singin' at the Rialto. Yimminy, what a girl!"

"I know." He went to his room. He had a notion to change clothes and find her that night. Instead, he went to bed. He didn't sleep well. He got up before daybreak, had breakfast with the crew, went back to his room, and shaved. His face was in better shape now. A lot better than that first night he saw her. He looked at his watch. Only 8:30

198

and Etty wasn't the type who got up before noon.

He stood at the high desk and looked at the surveyor's map that Dwight Gordon had sent him, showing the route of the spur line up Long Tom Gulch. Gordon wanted him to mark his loading point. He took half an hour in figuring it out and was just marking the X when he heard her voice in the next room. He strode over and opened the door.

"Buzz," she whispered, and the next instant she was clinging to him with her cheek pressed against his flannel shirt. "Buzz, you *are* glad to see me?"

She'd had a drink or two, and the smell of it, together with tobacco and perfume, brought back the memory of those Red Bank nights with jarring realism. Ole had come to the door with her and was staring, a grin on his moon face. Leary tried to let her go, but she cared nothing for what Ole thought.

"Oh, Buzz, why did you leave without saying anything? Why did you do it?"

He waited until Ole had backed out of sight and said: "I couldn't take you to Montreal. You must be able to understand that."

She was pouting again. "You didn't want to. You never really cared for me."

"You wouldn't want me if I was a quitter. What are you doing here in Skidway? Singing at the Rialto?"

"You know why I came. I came because of you."

She moved back a trifle, but still clung to him. "Buzz, I was here yesterday to see you. It was important. I wanted to warn you."

"What are you talking about?"

"They are planning to burn you out."

"Who?"

"I don't know. Somebody called Dardis. Some Dardis woman."

"How'd you find that out?"

"You hear things around places like the Rialto. Men get to drinking and they tell you more than they should. There was a man, a sawyer from the Dardis mill. He said his boss was going to burn you out."

"Franzen?"

"No, a woman. Mary Dardis. She was planning to burn you out."

Somebody had come to the door. Leary spun around and saw Mary Dardis. She was looking beyond him, at Etty.

"That's a lie!" Mary Dardis emphasized her words by hurling the door shut. She had a swaggering walk when she was angry, and she was angry now. She was dressed in wool shirt, Mackinaw, and stag trousers. The gun was strapped around her waist. She stopped with her hands on her hips, a couple of steps from Etty. "You heard what I said! I said it was a lie."

Etty was frightened. She whimpered something and got behind Leary.

Leary said: "Maybe it was a lie that your fore-man was here last night with a can of kerosene?"

She took a deep breath. She stood very straight, with her small shoulders back. Sunlight, coming through a smoky windowpane, brought out the flame color of her hair. By some magic, it looked darker, more like bronze, in daylight.

She said: "I wouldn't know about that. If he tried it, he was doing it on his own hook. *I* didn't send him. Anyhow, when I heard about it, I paid him off and gave him the boot. That's what I came here to tell you."

Etty, cringing behind Leary, whispered: "Don't believe her."

Mary heard her. "Say, who are you? Are you the new girl at the Rialto? I'll not be called a liar by any man in this camp, and it's a cinch I'll not take it from any dance-hall fluff."

Etty whispered: "It's true, Buzz. It is. She's the one who tried to burn you out. Don't let her fool you, Buzz."

He was watching Mary. He wondered what she'd do when she got mad enough. He wondered if she'd go for that gun at her waist. He kept his hands poised to grab her if she did.

She started forward, and he tried to push her back. She was quick as a forest cat. She dodged beneath his arm and seized Etty by the front of her jacket. Etty screamed and tried to claw her way free. She was no match for Mary's strength.

Mary kicked her feet from under her in the best timber-jack style, and tried to fling her to the floor. But in falling, Etty got hold of her hair with both hands.

They fell and rolled over and over. Fear had given Etty a desperate strength. She tore Mary's hair with one hand and tried to scratch her with the other. Mary got up far enough to swing her fist. She deliberately let the fist miss, doubled her elbow, and drove it to Etty's neck. Etty screamed and fell face down. She wasn't hurt that badly. She was screaming for Leary's sympathy. He stood over them, not knowing what to do.

Etty pushed herself up. She was on hands and knees with her hair spread out around her. Mary was on her feet now. She trampled on Etty's hair with her logger boots, pivoting with each step. Leary couldn't see the purpose in it, but he did when Etty tried to stand. Her hair was snagged in the slivery floor.

The girls had struggled for about half a minute. Finally Buzz Leary decided to take a hand. He grabbed Mary from behind, held her by her upper arms as she twisted back and forth. It was all he could do to hold her. Muscles, beneath the soft flesh of her arms, were like babiche thong. Her head was just under his chin. He could smell her hair. A fresh forest scent. Her shirt and Mackinaw had come open. He could see the white skin of her shoulder. He was strongly aware of her femininity. For a moment he forgot about Etty's harrowing plight on the floor. With a downward, twisting movement Mary got free. She whirled to face him. Her left hand clutched her shirt, holding the front of it closed. Her right, with a practiced swiftness, whipped the revolver from its holster.

"Mary!" he cried. "Be careful." Her finger was too hard on the trigger. Another ounce of pressure would bring the hammer back. "You better get out of here."

"Sure I will. I was a fool to come at all. Once a Leary, always a Leary." She strode over and looked down at Etty. Her feet were wide set, like they'd been when he first saw her at the Dardis mill office; the gun was at her side. "But before I do, I'd like to talk with this *friend* of yours."

Etty tried to turn her head and look up at her. Her eyes were like a frightened weasel's.

Mary said: "Now tell him the truth. Tell him you're a little plush-house liar."

"What?"

"Tell him you're a liar!"

"I'm a liar," she whimpered.

Mary turned away from her and said to Leary: "But you'll believe her, won't you? Sure you will . . . you dumb Irish timber tramp."

She strode out, coming down hard on the heels of her boots. He got down and helped pull Etty's hair loose. When she was free, she clutched his breast and sobbed: "But it was true! She made me say I was a liar. She really did send that man out to burn your mill."

Although he promised Etty he'd see her that night, instead he thought all day about Mary Dardis. He couldn't get over the impression of her closeness when he held her, the feel of her strong body, the fresh forest scent of her skin and hair. So that night, rather than going to the Rialto, he found himself once again walking toward the Dardis mill. No one fired at him this time. A lamp burned inside the house. He climbed the path across packed snow, rapped.

She drew up suddenly at seeing him. Her eyes moved beyond him, and for just a moment she seemed to be afraid.

"Well," she said, "what do you want?"

There was the defensiveness again. Her back was stiff and her little chin jutted out. The gun was strapped around her waist.

"I didn't want anything important. Just thought I'd drop around. Aren't many of us old-timers left. You, me, the Neils. Thought it over a long time and decided I'd find a better welcome here."

She said: "I made a fool of myself, didn't I?"

"Oh, I don't know." He touched his battered nose. "I didn't get that being smart. People that don't make fools of themselves aren't worth knowing."

"You really believe that?"

"Sure."

He followed her inside. She got the table between them and, with a return of tautness in her manner, said: "Is that why you believed that dance-hall girl instead of me?"

"You're not being fair. She thought you were to blame. You ought to admire her for trying to tell me the truth."

Mary made an exasperated gesture and her blue eyes started to dart fire. "She . . ." Mary checked herself. "I'll not say any more about her. You'll have to find out for yourself."

"That's generally how it is. Pa told me the whiskey would give me a headache, but I never believed him until I tried it."

The easy good humor of his talk had its effect, and she decided to smile. She said: "Well, are you a guest or on business?"

"Think I'd better be a guest."

"In that case, I'll pour a cup of tea."

"Coffee."

"Tea!"

While he drank, he knew she was watching him. After a long period of silence, with no sound except the snapping of knots in the stove, she spoke: "You don't think I tried to burn you out?"

"If I did, I don't suppose I'd be here." He put his cup aside. "I was thinking it'd still be a fine thing if you'd saw that Caribou pine of mine."

"Buzz, you'll never yard it. You'll never get those logs to Skidway, or anywhere."

"Yes, but what if I do?"

"No, I won't saw your timber." For a while she'd been a girl, soft and lovely. Now that was gone. Her little chin was out again. "Maybe *you're* right, Buzz. But the Learys broke my father and caused his death. I know that, Buzz. Everybody knows it. I'm not going into partnership with a Leary!"

He left an hour later and started for the Rialto, but Big Torg was on the street looking for him. He'd just arrived from Caribou with word that the Neils were hiring men away from the camp with higher wages. Leary countered by a raise topping the Neils. When it became apparent that a wage war would be too expensive, the Neils struck in a manner more direct. Their goon squad, led by huge, brutal Jug Claggett, commenced methodically beating every Leary man who showed up in town. They went afield, and waylaid men between Skidway and Caribou. The point was reached when few would take work with Leary at any wage, and he didn't blame them. Then he received word from Torg that the skidways between Caribou and Long Tom Gulch had been blasted. He realized that in some manner Oren Neil had learned the true destination of his timber.

Big Torg said: "We got to get that Claggett. Ay skal call my boys together. You give Swede axe handle, he fight like hell. Maybe we find two, three more. Johnny Bruce, he'll fight, and so will those Irishmen, McGraw and Callahan. Counting everyone, bane have eight. We'll catch Claggett down at the Rialto and . . ."

"I've thought of that, but he's wary as a two-toed wolf. He keeps showing himself alone, but when he gets jumped, those roughs come from everywhere. You get the boys together. I'll go down and see what I can find out."

Claggett was at the Rialto. Leary could see him through the front window—a huge, lumpy-faced man standing with one elbow on the bar and a bottle of beer in front of him. A couple of his men were there, too—Myers, and a big Finlander that Leary didn't know. The others were probably around, within shouting distance. He kept walking, waded snow around to the alley, climbed some outside stairs to the second story. He paused inside a hall and looked at the double row of rooms. Number 11, Etty had told him. He found it. Someone was moving around inside. He rapped, and she said: "Who is it?"

"Buzz."

He could hear her catch her breath. "Wait," she said. He stood a couple of minutes, then she let him in. Her white silk dress clung to the lines of her body. He had an idea she'd kept him waiting while she put it on. She grabbed his right hand in both of hers and drew him inside. "Buzz, why haven't you come before? And after you promised."

"They have me crowded against the wall. I haven't eaten since morning or slept more than four or five hours in the last two days."

He looked it, too. He'd lost weight since coming to Skidway. There was a set leanness in his jaw, a flinty look in his eyes. He got away from her and rested his long body on the edge of her dressing table.

She said: "What's wrong, Buzz? Is it Claggett?"

"Claggett and his toughs. They have the town buffaloed. It's getting so I can't hire a man."

"I heard they were blocking your rollways, too."

"Yes, but one thing at a time. I'm going to run Oren's bully boys out of town first, then I'll see about those fellows out in the hills."

"Oh, Buzz, I'm afraid. . . ."

She was going to cling to him again and he held her off with a long-thrust arm. "Wait. Do you really want to help me?"

"Yes! I'll do what I can . . . *anything* I can."

"All right. I'm getting some of my boys together. I want to catch Claggett when his knuckles crew is somewhere else. He hangs out here most of the time. Here at the Rialto. I want you to . . ."

"Yes, Buzz. I'll keep watch. Sometimes Neil takes most of them out of town with him. Last Thursday Claggett and Nakola were here, just the two of them, till midnight. Drunk, too. But if you get Claggett, you'll still have to deal with the others when . . ."

"Those timber toughs are all alike. Once they start getting their skulls kicked in, they hunt softer jobs a long way off. You send me word, Etty. How often does he let his guard down?"

"I don't know. It might be tonight. It might be a week."

He moved toward the door. "Etty, this means a lot to me."

She came to him and whispered: "Even Montreal?"

"Even Montreal. . . ."

Torg had the men together next afternoon. Among others, he'd recruited two Swede timber butchers named Rustad and Christianson from the Dardis mill. The addition of these brought the total to ten. Leary warned them they might be waiting for a good many days, but that evening the half-breed boy came with the message. It was written in a tiny hand on paper strong with Etty's perfume.

Only Claggett and four men here now. Others upriver. Hurry.

He sent the boy away, came back inside. The men stopped their poker game to watch him. He wadded the paper, threw it in the stove.

"That it?" Bruce asked.

"Yes." Leary looked at his watch. Seven o'clock. Claggett would have a bellyful of grub and the variety house crowd wouldn't be around yet. "Right now," he said.

He saw McGraw with a .45 Colt in his Mackinaw pocket and told him to leave it behind.

"How about axe handle?" Rustad asked. He was one of those Dardis Swedes. He'd been half drunk when he got there and had been spoiling for a fight all evening. "By yimminy, Ay can't fight wit'out chew snooce and axe handle."

"Go ahead and take it, but don't swing it unless they start swinging 'em first. I don't want anybody killed. I want 'em alive so they can tell how bad this country is for timber toughs."

# IV

The street looked quiet with the thermometer at zero and light from the saloon windows shining brightly across the new snow.

Leary stopped and said: "Torg, you take the Swedes down that side. Bruce, you keep your boys across the street. When the ruckus starts, I want about four men outside. They might have a deadfall fixed up for us."

Bruce said: "What about you?"

"I'll go over there."

"Alone?"

"Sure." He made an impatient gesture when Torg started to object. "Keep watch. I might need help in a hurry."

He started toward the Rialto, making a long slant across the street. He was halfway when Mary Dardis called him. He spun around and saw her coming down the steps from the Northern Mercantile Company. She came across, taking rapid steps, and stopped to look up at him, her head tilted to one side. Her eyes lacked their fire tonight. They looked scared.

She said, her voice unusually soft and pleading: "Buzz, you're headed for trouble. You're headed for more trouble than you can handle."

He let his shoulders jerk with a laugh. "It might surprise you how much trouble I can handle."

"That girl is going to double-cross you."

"Think she'll have Neil waiting for us?"

"I don't know a thing about that. All I know is you have a couple of my men, drunk and ready to get their heads beaten in, and I don't like it."

"Talk to them, not me. They're over twenty-one."

"How do you reason with a drunken Swede?"

"How do you reason with a sober Irishman? One's as bad as the other." Then he dropped the grin off his face and said: "It would please every drop of ornery Dardis blood you got to see me fold up and get run out of the country, wouldn't it?"

"You'll get run out. Etty and Oren will see to that."

He watched her spin on her toe and walk off. There were Etty and Oren Neil tied together again. He recalled what the old fellow in Red Bank had said. And something else had been in the back of his mind—that survey map had been lying open on his desk the morning Etty visited him, and right afterward Neil moved to block his route to Long Tom Gulch.

He walked on to the Rialto's front sidewalk. The windows were steamed over. He waited for the door to open and got a glimpse of the interior. Not many around yet. Claggett, Myers, and a couple others were sitting around a disused card table. He decided not to go in after all, circled to the rear, climbed the stairs. He listened for a while in the lamplit hall, and walked to Etty's room. She was there. He turned the knob, opened the door.

She said—"Oren!"—and whirled. She caught herself then, and tried to laugh. She had a silk robe tied around her. It came to the floor and made her look smaller than ever. She took a provocative tuck in it and came to him, saying: "Oh, Buzz, the idea you must have of me! I was thinking about *him,* Oren Neil, and the night he kicked you in the face so awfully. I was worried about tonight, and then the door coming open . . ."

"Sure." He closed the door with the heel of his hobbed boot. "Sure, I know." He noticed that her

212

lips were smiling, but her eyes were as shifty as a mink's. She tried to snuggle up to him as she had so many times in the past. He looked over her head and saw a cigar burned out in her dressing table ashtray. "Where is he?"

"Who?"

He pushed her out of his way, took a long step, and jerked the closet curtain aside. Nobody there. He turned then and said: "You know who . . . Oren Neil?"

"Oh, Buzz! Buzz, you don't really think . . . ?"

"I think you tried to make a punk out of me in Red Bank. Tried to get me to sell the Caribou to Oren Neil."

"Buzz. . . ." Her shoulders shook convulsively and she tried to bury her face in the front of his shirt.

"What's he giving you?" He grabbed her, shoved her back. "What's he giving you?"

Suddenly she stopped pretending. Her little mouth was drawn thin and turned down at the corners, twisted, contemptuous. She bared her teeth and almost spat at him. "You fool! You ugly fool! Do you think I'd give you a second look unless I had a reason for it? Do you think any woman would choose you instead of Oren? Of course, I made a fool of you. In Red Bank and here in Skidway, too. I got inside your office and you let me see the very thing Oren wanted most to know. And I told him. Oh, how he sat here and laughed, when I told him. And about you, you big stumbling punk . . . you and your poor Etty stuff. I wanted to tell you to go to hell then, but Oren said to hold off a while and get you good. He said he didn't dare get too rough, not with you having the railroad behind you. He said maybe you'd come looking for trouble. And you did. You came pussyfooting to me. Promising maybe you'd take me to Montreal."

He'd never hit a woman. He started and checked himself. Frightened, she screamed: "Oren! He's here, Oren!"

He tried to stop her. She kept screaming. He could hear heavy boots in the hall. The door flew open, and Oren Neil was there.

Neil came to a stop. A huge man, he filled the doorway. Back of him was Bill, and skinny-faced Lyn LaValley, owner of the Rialto. Etty was shrieking, telling him things, but Neil didn't look at her. He backhanded her out of the way and said: "Well, Leary! So this is the place you picked for it." He laughed, his head tossed back, hands on his hips. Then he stopped and the laugh seemed to leave a vile taste in his mouth. "It suits me, Leary. It suits me fine."

Leary said: "Where are your guts?"

"Now what did you mean by that?"

"I mean you haven't the guts to fight me without Bill and that sneaking LaValley at your back."

"Teach you that in the hockey arena? Even up

214

and all sporting, old topper? I fight to win. That's what I'm going to do tonight. I'm going to cave your skull in. And everybody knows you came here with your mob looking for it."

Leary had backed a step away. His left hand was behind him, on the back of a chair. A kerosene lamp was burning on the dressing table at his right. He said—"Sure, Oren."—and picked up the lamp.

LaValley shouted—"Look out!"—just as Leary threw it.

It struck the wall, shattered. The room was dark, a darkness filled with the fumes of kerosene. He'd expected the kerosene to set the wall afire and drive them all out, but it didn't. A second later, Oren and Bill both charged him. Light from the hall gave him a vague impression of movement. He shifted his position, wielding the heavy chair.

He met Oren Neil with the full force of it and dropped him in one direction. With a return movement he smashed Bill. He ran against Etty. She screamed—"Here he is!"—and clung to his arm. He tried to rip free. She hung with the clawing ferocity of a cat. He came around with all his strength and snapped her free. She struck the floor and Oren Neil, rising, trampled her. She wailed his name and he cursed her, booted her out of the way.

Leary turned with the chair to meet him but in the darkness Bill staggered head foremost into it.

It dropped him so hard the floor shook. He came up, made a blind grab for Leary's knees, but he took a hobnail boot between the eyes and went down like he'd been blackjacked. Leary lit on him and gave him the hobs. He saw Oren coming with a bull charge. The man's superior weight carried him to the hall. There the hobs on Leary's left heel caught the carpet and he fell backward, caught himself on his hands. Oren went for him with his boots, but this time Leary wasn't the easy prey he'd been on the corduroy walks of Red Bank.

He rolled, felt one of the boots graze his face. Neil tried to turn. Leary rose from beneath him, caught him by his crotch and the front of his shirt, and lifted him high in the air, trying to drive his head against the ceiling. Neil twisted over, fingers hunting for Leary's eyes. His struggling weight carried Leary off balance. He took three lunging, running steps, fell but, in falling, managed to propel the man headforemost down the narrow stairway.

He could hear cursing and the *crash* of a handrail. Some of those timber toughs had been coming upstairs and Oren Neil's plunging body had taken them down again. A knife pain went through Leary's knee and he steadied himself with his back against the wall. His leg still held him, but he'd have to go easy on it. Then Oren Neil charged back into sight.

He had a segment of banister. A heavy oaken

club. He grasped it with both hands and wielded it like a ball bat. Leary moved enough to take it across an upflung arm. A glancing blow. He went to one knee and kept going forward. Oren Neil thought he was going down, backed away half a step, and started a second swing. He saw it would miss and tried to change its direction. Leary let it graze his shoulder, hesitated a fraction of a second with his heels set, and smashed a right to his jaw. It stunned big Oren Neil. His eyes were off focus like the eyes of a beef under a slaughterhouse hammer. He reeled, hit the wall with his shoulder. His weight crushed lath and plaster. He rebounded as his legs folded under him. He sat down hard, but he wasn't out; he had enough left to get one arm as a shield and grope with his club for the other.

Leary did not hesitate. He'd been raised in the big timber and knew the rules under which the timber jack fights. A man is put down only to make him vulnerable to the real weapons—the boots on one's feet. He sprang when Neil was lunging to his feet. The hobs raked him and carried him down again. Neil rolled over, got up. He didn't realize the stairs were behind him. He fell backwards and rolled to the landing. Leary was atop him in two long steps. Neil stood and was smashed down the next six steps by a right and left to the jaw. He was groggy but not quite out. There was a baffled, beaten look in his eyes.

His face was smashed. He coughed and spat out a tooth. His lips moved but the words were drowned out by riot in the saloon beyond.

"You had enough?" Leary asked.

He nodded his head.

Leary seized him by the shirt front and flung him away. His head clumped the wall and he pitched face forward, limp and beaten. Leary stepped over him and reached the lower stair landing that overlooked the saloon and gambling room. It was full of struggling, chair-swinging men. The fight had passed its apex. The place was a shambles, bar overturned, mirrors smashed, faro and roulette spreads heaped against the walls. He could see and hear Big Torg over everyone, a chair in his hands, mowing through the last remnants of Claggett's timber toughs.

Claggett had his men all there, and a few Neil lumberjacks to boot. They should have had Leary's bunch outnumbered. It took him a moment to realize that most of the wrecking crew were from the Dardis camps. They were tough, too. He saw Mary at the door and started toward her. A stray chair struck him on the shoulder and bounded off. He scarcely looked around. Big Torg rammed him out of the way. He was dragging Jug Claggett by the collar. He dumped him at Mary's feet and commenced booting him in the ribs.

"You talk, noo!" he roared. "Talk! Talk!" he repeated, kicking him a little harder each time.

218

"You talk. Tell Mary Dardis who bane kill her father. You talk or Ay skal cave in planty more ribs."

"I'll talk." Jug usually affected a swaggering voice and manner, but tonight he was reduced to a cringing whine. "I'll talk. Leave me alone, I'll talk. It wasn't me. I didn't have anything to do with it. It was a long time ago, and . . ."

"Talk!"

"He come up and Bill hit him. He'd have let it go at that. He ain't like Oren. He's mean, but he's not crazy. But Oren always hated your dad, and he jumped on him with his boots, and . . ."

"That's enough," Leary said. "Save it for the police when we get them here from Fort Royal."

Mary said: "I want to hear it."

"That's all I know. He got him with his hobs eight or ten times before Bill could drag him off. He's got an awful temper, Oren has. He goes crazy. I don't know if he intended to kill your dad. He was scared afterward. They had Hobs Donahue tied up and Oren talked about killing him, too, so he couldn't talk. But he thought it over and decided nobody would believe Hobs anyhow. So he turned Hobs loose and told him to hit the skids out o' here. I'd have told. I'd have gone to the law, only them Neil boys would have . . ."

"All right," Mary said.

Leary took her outside. Men were still running

that way to see the excitement. He led her down the snow-covered walks. He was bare-headed, his shirt ripped open. The zero breeze felt good. It washed him of that rotten combination of sweat, whiskey, and perfume that filled the Rialto.

"I've been a fool," he said. "I should have known Franzen was in with the Neils when he tried to burn me. I should have known he was working with them when he tossed that Winchester lead at me that first evening when I went up to the mill."

She asked about Oren and Bill Neil, and he told her. He noticed that her chin was no longer jutted. Her fear and defensiveness were gone.

One of her hands rested on his arm. He took hold of her arms, just below her shoulders, turned her so she was facing him. He didn't know he was going to kiss her. He didn't know her head would be tilted back, that her lips would be waiting for him.

He said: "I still have a lot of white pine and no mill to put it through."

"We'll make a business appointment some-time." She was smiling up at him. He was surprised to see her eyes swimming through tears. "Who wants to talk about the lumber business now, you big, dumb Irishman, you?"

# BURNED WITH THE
# COYOTE BRAND

# I

Axel Colbon and his daughter set out at noon for the long drive to the Vintner Creek schoolhouse. The girl chattered with nervous gaiety most of the time, now and then standing to shake out her new dress and admire its colors by the bright Montana sunshine. Sometimes she would glance at her father as though expecting him to admire the dress, too, but he always looked straight ahead, taking the jolts of the rig with an unyielding spine. His body had a tense angularity accentuated by his store clothes that had obviously been put away for many years and now hung on him with unnatural folds.

"Do you suppose the Gradys will be there, Axel?" Loney Colbon always called her father by his first name.

"Why, yes, I suppose so." Colbon spoke in the thoughtful, measured manner of men who converse infrequently. Then he repeated, as though to assure himself on a vital point: "Yes, I guess the Gradys will sure enough be there."

"And the Hoffstables? And the Wigginses?"

"The Wigginses, anyhow."

"And who else?"

"Oh . . . a bunch of the Milliron 'punchers, and Jim Smith, and I suppose most of the Steckley outfit."

Loney glanced quickly at her father as he pronounced that name: "Steckley." She waited as though expecting more but he lapsed into his old, silent rigidity. Loney's mother, Tania, had run off with one of the Steckleys long ago and Axel scarcely ever mentioned them. Months, even years, would go by, and, if Axel ever had cause to speak of the vast Steckley domain, he would call it the "S Diamond" or the "Flying W." Actually it had helped Axel to pronounce that name—Steckley—and it would have helped him more to talk about Tania, but he didn't. He kept his eyes straight ahead, over the backs of his ill-matched cayuse team on crisp brown bench land.

Until that morning the memory of Tania had been like a wound healed over with the bullet inside to ache only now and then, when the weather was bad. And then Loney put on that new dress from the mail-order house. It had the gaudy colors and cheap frills that Tania loved. He had watched her as she stood and danced tiptoe in front of the rusty mirror—like her mother all over again. His face had gone hard, and he walked out to hitch the broncos to the buggy.

Tania wasn't her real name. Her real name had been Mary, but she had changed it to Tania after reading a French love story. Axel Colbon had met her at a dance at the old Baker Ranch on the Judith. She had come with Jack Dorrence, but Axel's handsome recklessness had carried her off her feet, and next day they rode forty miles in to Fort Benton to be married.

Colbon had owned a few longhorns, a house with no floor in it, and $1,000,000 worth of hope. They had been happy a few weeks, but Tania had dreamed of something different. Loney was born, but she didn't help. Tania would sit whole days at a time, staring across the treeless swale of Arrow Creek. And one day she ran away with Walt Steckley whose father owned the S Diamond and could buy plenty of houses with floors in them.

Axel Colbon had not followed to shoot it out with Walt as the country's standards of honor assumed that he would. Walt was a hard, supremely confident fellow, deadly with firearms, and Axel had a year-old baby to think about. If folks wanted to call him a coward, that was their privilege. He stayed home, raised the kid, and tried to make something of his two-bit ranch.

That had been sixteen years ago, and, although he had been forced into Walt's company at roundup time, he had managed not to see Tania once. Then, a month ago, he heard that Walt and Tania were moving to old Roose Steckley's Flying W over north, and Loney had been begging to go to this dance.

The wagon trail wound with slow curves across the bench land and at last tilted toward Vintner Creek whose valley was already gathering the purple shadows of sunset. There were lamps burning in the schoolhouse when they jolted the last couple of miles across the creek bottoms.

Axel drew up, keeping his bronco team from trotting the last 100 yards, while he peered through the gathering dusk to see if Walt Steckley's top buggy was among the rigs already arrived. It wasn't. Some of the tenseness dropped away from him then. He turned to Loney and smiled.

"Looks like most of the folks are here."

She nodded eagerly, sitting very straight, holding the seat of the buggy.

"Waal, shoot me for a Blackfoot, look who shows up for the shindig!" yipped old Wes Geary, range boss of the Milliron outfit. "There's Ax Colbon crawled out of his hole for the first time in a month of Februarys!"

Axel Colbon climbed down and shook hands around. He felt self-conscious, coming to a dance after so many years. A couple of Geary's cow-punchers unhitched the team. Colbon went inside, hung his gun and cartridge belt on a peg, and his hat over them. He glanced around the long schoolroom. Neither Walt nor Tania were there, of course. Dad Banks was seated in a chair on the teacher's desk, fiddling. Axel watched a cowboy grab Loney for the quadrille. She seemed so different out there in her bright new dress when he had grown used to seeing her in Levi's and blue shirt. He went outside.

Geary had a keg of bullberry wine in the box of his Dempster wagon. Axel sampled it. Considerable time must have slipped away for it was dark with no hint of sunset when a word made him jerk suddenly and listen. Someone had called out that name: "Steckley." He drew another cupful from the keg, trying to conceal the tremble in his arm. Tania and Walt Steckley had come after all—he was sure of it.

The thought of Tania's being there so close was like a wound from a dull knife. And his hatred of Walt Steckley, too. He wanted to hitch up and go home, but he was drawn to the window to look inside.

Tania was the first person he saw. She was in the dancing circle—older but still beautiful. It hurt him to see how much Loney took after her. And there was Walt Steckley, too.

Walt was a large, raw-boned man of about thirty-eight, which was Axel's age, although a stranger would have guessed Axel to be ten years the elder. Walt was handsome and smiling, his face perspiring from the speed of the dance.

Loney was over in the far circle. Her partner—Axel Colbon stood straight, frozen-faced, as a cold, frustrated fury filled him. Her partner was young Tom Steckley, Walt's half-brother.

Tom Steckley was not so large as Walt. He lacked Walt's swagger, his long aggressive jaw. A stranger would have called his face likable but that quality only made Axel hate him more.

The dance ended and Tom Steckley was taking Loney back to the bench by the wall. She held his arm and was looking at him, laughing. The same eager expression Axel had seen on her mother's face seventeen years ago. He cursed and started toward the schoolhouse door.

"Axel!" It was round-faced Wes Geary. "Take it easy, Ax. It's only a dance. Tom Steckley ain't a bad kid."

"You mind your business and I'll mind mine."

"Good God, can't you forget something that happened nigh onto twenty year ago?"

Axel paused, the palm of his right hand rubbing that place at his hip where his scabbard generally hung. He turned and strode on inside, almost running into Tania. She stared at him, started to speak, but he looked right through her and walked on. Walt stood at one side and watched with eyes hard as gray flint, the corners of his mouth twisted down.

Everyone had been talking at once, and then, abruptly, the room was so quiet that the *clump* of his boot heels could be heard on the plank floor.

"Loney!"

She looked up. The flushed smile drained from her face.

"Come along!"

She had a tight grip on the sleeve of Tom's shirt and seemed too frozen with surprise to let loose.

Tom looked at her. At her father. "You're Axel Colbon," he said. "I remember you . . . you were repping for the badlands spreads up on the Milk River roundup when I was . . ."

"I know who you are," snapped Colbon.

"You mean you won't let Loney stay because she was dancing with a Steckley?"

"If I ever see you with my daughter again, I'll kill you." He spoke his next words more loudly so Walt Steckley, and even old Roose over in the corner, would be sure to hear. "I've taken enough from your breed and I'm not going to take any more!"

"That was aimed at me, wasn't it?" asked Walt. He walked up a few steps, his arms long and loose, only the sinuous sway of his back and shoulders hinting at the spring-steel quality of his strength.

"Yes, it was aimed at you!"

"Not in here, fellows!" The caller jumped down from the teacher's platform and spoke pleadingly. "If there's going to be any trouble, go outside."

Walt said: "I'm tired of you, Colbon. I'm tired of your sulking. I'm sick of the lies you've spread about me. I wouldn't have taken them from anyone else, but I felt sorry for you and let it go. I've let you make a living and fatten your cows on Steckley grass. But I'm through. Now get going while you still have a hide to cover you."

Walt was fifty pounds heavier—a superb physical specimen. Axel knew he would have no

229

chance with his fists. His gun was on the peg. He could see the scabbard and a few inches of his cartridge belt hanging beneath his Stetson. Walt carried no belt and holster, but Axel's blind rage sent him for the gun anyway.

Walt did not move. He waited, a smile twisting his lips. The front of his coat was open, his hand there. At that second Axel knew that Walt had deliberately enraged him for this purpose, to make him go for his gun, and then kill him with a perfect excuse of self-defense. He knew he was practically a dead man, but there was nothing to do but go on.

Axel grabbed the scabbard with his left hand, his right closed on the sweat-blackened butt of his .45. People were shouting and stampeding out of the way. There was a silvery flash from the front of Walt's coat as he wheeled the hide-away from its shoulder holster.

"Walt!" Tom Steckley screamed at him.

Walt tried to fend off his brother with his left hand and draw down. Tom set his heels and swung with all the lean snap of his young body. He connected with Walt's jaw, sending him spinning backward. Walt collided with the wall, bounded, went to hands and knees with the silver-plated .32 *clattering* across the plank floor. Axel had drawn his six-gun, but Tom was in the way. He held it, cocked. He conquered an obvious temptation to shoot, lowered the hammer, buckled the cartridge belt around his lean waist, and dropped the Colt in the holster.

Walt sat up, shaking his powerful head. His eyes were bloodshot with hatred, fastened, not on Axel, but on his half-brother. He started up from the floor, but his father, old Roose Steckley, had hobbled over on his rheumatically shriveled legs, his diamond-willow walking stick hammering the floor.

"Walt!"

Roose Steckley's voice snapped like a bull-whip. It was the voice of a man who had always commanded—the only voice on earth that could have stopped Walt then. Walt, with a visible effort, controlled himself.

"Walt, get your rig hitched and go home!" said Roose.

"Sorry, Walt," Tom said.

"Sure, kid." Walt tried to smile, but there was nothing easy about smiling at a fellow when you've always hated his guts.

# II

Tom Steckley stayed at the dance until old Roose was ready to go home. He hitched the team of grays to the buckboard and drove north and west to the valley of Rock Creek where the Steckley home ranch lay. Old Roose didn't have much to say most of the distance, but when Tom drew up in front of the ranch house, he spoke.

"Stay out of Walt's way for a while, Tom. He's like his mother . . . venom enough to burn the bottom off a brass kettle, but he'll get over it. And stay away from that Colbon girl. I guess Axel's taken enough from us Steckleys already."

Tom helped him down, and the old man went inside, pounding his diamond-willow walking stick on the floor each time he swung his stove-up right leg.

Tom had tried to sleep but the excitement had been too much for him. He got up and stood in the warm early sunlight that flooded the porch along the east side of the old ranch house. Down below he could see several acres of corrals made of aspen poles, the bunkhouse with dirt roofs where weeds had taken root, the big barn where Roose had kept the driving teams when his second wife, Tom's mother, was alive. It all looked disreputable and run-down, and not like the thing it was—the center of a cattle empire.

Across Arrow Creek, on a shoulder of land, he could see the mounds of a prairie dog town. Tom sometimes sat on the porch and shot the pests with his .30-30. He got the gun from his saddle scabbard, but he pumped the cartridges from the magazine and shot dry in deference to old Roose who was sleeping in the corner room.

A couple of riders were coming up the creek trail from the Culver place. The Culver place had been part of the ranch ever since old Roose froze Jeff Culver out twenty-five years ago, but it still wore the name. Walt had been living there with Tania for the last five years.

The posture of the riders told him that one was Walt, and the other was Cal Lotts, drifter from points south who Walt had hired for "special jobs" over the objections of Roose a couple of years before. Walt left Cal Lotts by the cook house and jolted on across the hard-beaten ranch yard to the porch.

"Keeping your hand in?" he asked, his face immobile, and only his eyes revealing his resentment of this half-brother of his, this son of a money-grabbing mother who would someday come in for half the Steckley property.

Tom lowered the rifle and smiled. "Sure."

"That thing doesn't throw a scare into me."

"I didn't intend it to."

"Then why did you get it down when you saw me coming?"

Tom pumped the lever mechanism several times to show that the magazine was empty. Walt ignored the action. He dropped the quirt end of his bridle and *clomped* inside the house, letting his spurs drag after the manner of heavy-legged men. He looked for Roose, and then came out. Tom was snapping at the prairie dogs again.

233

"You probably think you're quite a man after last night," said Walt.

"What do you mean?"

"Putting your big brother on the floor."

"Hell, Walt, forget about it. What good would it do you to kill Axel Colbon?"

"Why didn't you hit Axel instead of me?"

"You know why. Because you were ready to . . ."

"Because you were on his side. Because you have a crush on that girl. And maybe you think Colbon is in the right! Is that it? Do you think he's in the right?"

Tom wanted to ask Walt if he was troubled by a bad conscience but he held his peace. He didn't want to go against old Roose's warning, and it was true that deep inside him he had a little fear of this elder half-brother.

"Forget it," he said.

"Sure. I don't hold anything against you for that little poke on the jaw. Only don't get too big for your britches." He paused and grinned. "Someday I'm going to take time to find out just how much of a man you are."

Walt swung his leg over and sawed on the mean, half-breed bit he always used. There was smoke coming from the cook house stovepipe and Walt headed there. Tom followed a few minutes later. Only a handful of cowpunchers had crawled out for grub pile. Cal Lotts had finished breakfast and sat with one spur digging the bench,

234

talking about people he "had a good notion to kill." That was all Lotts cared to talk about—killing.

Lotts was a tall, run-over-looking man of thirty or so. He was slovenly, and bucktoothed, and he had a habit of letting his mouth droop open that accounted for his behind-the-back nickname of "Fishface."

Walt said: "Cal, I'm going to send Tom and Blamey out to help you drift those cattle over."

Cal Lotts nodded. He generally growled when told to work cattle. The only kind of job he really enjoyed was running some helpless sodbuster off Steckley range. But on this occasion he seemed actually pleased. Tom decided there was something more than riding connected with it.

"What cattle are they?" he asked, but Walt pretended not to hear. Walt ate, shoveling his breakfast half a pancake at a time, then he *clomped* outside. "What cattle was he talking about, Cal?"

Lotts sucked on the soggy stump of a cigarette and let the smoke drift between his buckteeth. He didn't like authority, and this delay was one of his ways of digging the old man's son.

"Why, I thought Walt just told you."

"You know damned well he didn't."

"Then how should I know what cattle they are? I don't sleep in the big house."

"You're too damned smart, Lotts. Somebody will take it out of you one of these days."

235

"Maybe you?"

"I'm not afraid of you or the guns you carry. I've seen other men talk kill all the time, and then show the coyote brand when the cards were dealt."

Lotts grinned. "You *know* you're the boss' son, don't you?"

Blamey, a short, red-faced cowpuncher, spoke to break it up: "It's those Mexican steers that Walt bought off the Canadian drive. He aims to get them off the Vintner Crick range to better grass on Arrow Bench so's he can ship 'em this fall."

The clash with Lotts left Tom a trifle upset. He tried to eat pancakes, but he couldn't stomach them, so he drank coffee and went outside. Lotts came out a minute later, grinning like a well-fed cat.

"Forget it, Tommy boy. If I ever fought with you, it would be just plain murder and I don't aim to stiffen a rope for a while yet."

That day the three men set out for the Vintner Creek range with a bob-tailed cavvy and a pack horse. It would take them a couple or three days to drift the 900 Mexican cattle to the Arrow bench. In that time the hooligan wagon would get over to the line shack and leave grub. The three men would have to stay on to keep the steers from drifting down on Axel Colbon's range. The grass on the bench proved to be fair but Tom could see it was nothing to stack up tallow on a steer's ribs.

A week passed, and the three men got along well

enough. From the line shack on the bench Tom could look across the valley of the Arrow and see Colbon's place, perfect in miniature, nine or ten miles away. He kept watch through the field glasses for a glimpse of Loney, for he did not risk the wrath of her father by riding down to visit her.

One afternoon he noticed that Cal's end of the herd had drifted down across the Arrow range. Cal was nowhere around, so Tom rode down after them. He met Loney riding up from the ranch.

She looked a lot different today than she had back at the dance. No frills and ruffles—she was dressed like a boy in blue shirt and Levi's and tiny, run-over riding boots. Her hair had been roached and the long ends tucked beneath the floppy Stetson hat that Jim Coyne, the 69 renegade rider, had left at Colbon's ranch three years ago. She was brown, and supple, and somehow Tom Steckley liked her even better than he had at the dance.

Loney drew up a dozen yards away and cried accusingly: "Dad said you'd be driving those steers down on our grass . . . and you have!"

"We didn't drive 'em down, Loney. Fact is, there's three of us here just to keep 'em from coming down. One of the boys got to sleeping with his chaps on, I guess."

He let his horse graze for a while, satisfied just to sit and look at her. Loney tried to nurse her indignation, but it wasn't easy with Tom so good-natured.

She said: "Axel would make it plenty hot for you if he rode up."

"There's a dance over at the Milliron barn Saturday after next. Reckon you can go?"

"Not after last week. Axel wouldn't . . ."

"I'll ride and fetch you."

"And get shot!"

"Not after I swatted Walt down just for his benefit."

"Axel says you just did that to save Walt from hanging. . . ."

"You don't believe that, do you, Loney?"

She shook her head.

"Then I'll ride over and fetch an extra horse. Your pa does more bellerin' than buttin'."

"No, Tom. You don't know how he feels toward all you Steckleys. He never forgets anything. He just stores it away inside. He doesn't talk about it, but still it's there. Do you know he hasn't mentioned my mother five times that I can remember? When I used to ask about her, he'd walk out of the house. He meant it about killing you. . . ."

"Maybe. But he'll back down when it comes to pulling the trigger. Where's he now?"

"Over riding the breaks."

Axel Colbon spent a good share of his time mavericking out in the breaks where the roundup didn't touch, and every year he turned up with a herd of ten-year-olds so tough they were good for little except boot soles. His range didn't amount to much.

She said: "You'd better get those steers back to the bench before he sees them."

With Loney's help, Tom worked them away from the Arrow. It was a slow job, and they were still at it when Axel rode up the old Army trail from the breaks. He came across, taking the jolts of his horse against a stiff spine, waiting until he was close before he spoke.

"Go back to the house, Loney."

"No!"

"I said go to the house!"

Reluctantly she turned her horse. After forty or fifty yards she drew the horse to a stop and sat watching over her shoulder. Her father saw her there, but said nothing.

Tom rolled a quirly. "We didn't *drive* those steers down on you, Colbon," he said, lighting and flipping the match away.

Axel spoke slowly, controlling his voice: "You Steckleys have got me where you want me . . . pinned between you and the breaks. I suppose this looks like a good time to freeze me out. But let me tell you this . . . I'll shoot every Steckley cow I see on my range after tomorrow morning."

"Take it easy, Axel. We're not . . ."

"And stay away from Loney. I don't know

what kind of lies you filled her ear with Saturday night, but she hasn't been herself since. And it all adds up to misery. I'll never let a Steckley have her."

"You can't tell Loney what to do any more than you could tell one of those wild antelope out in the breaks. When she sees a man she wants, she'll have him."

"It won't be you."

"Why, I guess that's up to Loney. I'm ridin' down to take her to the dance at the Milliron on Saturday after next . . . if she'll go with me."

"You're carrying a gun today!"

"But I ain't goin' for it, and you aren't goin' for yours. If you shot me, she'd hate you the rest of your days. You ain't takin' a chance on Loney . . . and neither am I."

Axel Colbon sat there, his face as tough and expressionless as Cree leather, but something about his posture, a little droop in his axe-handle spine, showed that he knew Tom Steckley was right. He could never shoot the man Loney cared for.

"You keep your damned stock off the Arrow!" he said.

"Dad's not trying to freeze you out, Colbon. And neither am I. I can't guarantee but what a few strays will come down, but, if they do, it's an accident. This herd will be held on the bench. You got *my* word for it."

Cal Lotts rode down to help drive the cattle back to bench land. He didn't say much, but a smile on his droopy mouth was evidence that he had enjoyed the scene from above.

# III

It was evening, two days later, and the three men were at the line shanty finishing supper when Charley Jesrud, the Steckley outrider, came over from the home ranch with word that old Roose had suffered a stroke.

"He's restin' easy, but he can't recognize anybody," Charley said. "Walt says for you three boys to come right in."

"We can't all go," Tom told him. "We have to hold these steers."

"I'm just tellin' you what he said."

"Well, what Walt says is good enough for me," Lotts remarked, casting a sidelong glance at Tom. "If the boss says come in, I come in, cattle or not."

"You're staying here to ride herd," Tom said.

"Walt is my boss!"

"I own as big an interest in this ranch as . . ."

"Don't order me around, Tommy boy, because I ain't the type that takes to it."

He was standing beside the table, his mouth twisted in that loose, sneering smile that Tom had learned to detest. To add point, he hooked his right thumb in one of his cartridge belts and gave it a *snap*. Tom wasn't much at hiding his emotions, and the anger on his face made Cal expect him to go for his gun. In that case, no doubt Cal would have killed him, for he was riding high now with Roose down and Walt in the saddle. Instead, Tom took a quick step forward and swung a sledge-hammer right.

The move was a surprise. The gunman's head snapped back so violently his hat spun from his head. He struck the wall so hard the flimsy shack *creaked*. He was down with his head against the wall, staring like a pike, a thin dribble of spit and blood coming from his loose mouth.

For a second or two he was like that, then he rolled, freeing his right-hand scabbard. Even stunned as he was, and in a bad position, his draw proceeded like the action of some automatic mechanism. But the quarters were too close. Tom swung his foot, booting the gun out of his hand.

Lotts staggered to his feet, spitting blood. Tom kicked the loose gun over the sill into the deep, white dust outside the door. Lotts followed after it, stumbling over his own toes. He picked it up and very carefully slid it back in his scabbard, for he knew that Tom was in there with his own gun half drawn. He did not look back, but ambled unsteadily over to the cavvy to saddle a horse.

"You're going to have plenty of trouble with that killer before you're through," said Charley Jesrud.

Blamey asked Tom: "You goin' in to the ranch?"

"I have to."

"How the devil am I goin' to hold these nine hundred wild Mexicans? It was all the three of us could do. There isn't more'n a week left in most of these bench water holes, and, when they dry up, all hell and General Grant couldn't keep 'em away from Arrow Crick."

"Charley, you stay and help."

"I can't do it. I have to grab me a fresh horse and flag across the river to fetch the Willards."

The Willards were Walt's cousins on his mother's side. They were a trashy bunch, and the Willard men fancied themselves as fighters.

"Then you'll have to stay here alone, Blamey, and do the best you can."

"Walt said for Blamey to go in, too."

"And I say for him to stay!"

"I don't want to get in trouble with Walt," Blamey grumbled. "I better go on in, and you can send somebody else out tomorrow. Them cattle are pretty deep. They won't move as far as the Arrow before sundown."

"You stay here."

Blamey stood disconsolately in the door, watching, while Tom and Charley Jesrud saddled.

"I'll send a couple of the boys out in the

243

morning!" Tom shouted over his shoulder as he rode off into the twilight toward Rock Creek.

He got to the ranch next morning just as Doc MacArdle was sitting down to breakfast.

"He spent a good night," the doc said. "Go on in and see him. He won't recognize you."

"Is there any hope?"

"You know how strokes are. Once in a while they pull through, but they never get entirely all right. This one's pretty bad."

Old Roose lay in the brass bed, eyes closed, breathing heavily. Mary Loboz, a practical nurse from Grass Valley, was with him. Tom stood around for a while, wondering what he should do. He went back to the big room and drank a cup of coffee with MacArdle. Through a smoked-up side window he could see Walt's horse saddled down by the bunkhouse. He walked down.

Walt saw him and came out. "Well, kid, it looks like it was all up with the gov'nor."

He was impassive, standing there, his stud-horse legs spread solidly, his heavy fingers plucking grass stickers from the sleeve of his shirt.

Tom said: "Those steers are over there at the edge of the Arrow. Blamey can't handle them all alone."

"I told Blamey to come back to the ranch. Why didn't he?"

"Because I told him to stay."

Walt stopped picking at the sleeve of his shirt.

His eyes went hard. He clenched and unclenched his right fist. "Since when did you take over?"

"I haven't taken over, but you can't turn those steers loose to run over the Arrow range."

"Why?"

"You know damned well why. Because that's Colbon's grass."

"It's Steckley grass. Colbon squatted on it twenty years ago and I've been an easy mark and never run him off. But I'm through handling that fellow with a cloth rope."

"Roose doesn't want any more trouble with Colbon. He said . . ."

"I'm roddin' the outfit now, Tommy, and it would pay you not to forget it."

"I promised Colbon our cattle wouldn't drift down on . . ."

"Then you promised him too damned much."

"He swears he'll shoot every steer that comes down there."

"If he shoots one of my steers, I'll sue him for everything he owns. And if that doesn't turn the trick, I guess there are other ways of taking care of him."

Tom could see why Walt had sent him over there with those Mexican steers. He wanted to get him in trouble with Colbon. And now that Roose was headed for the Great Divide, he was coming out in the open. He intended to drive Colbon into the badlands.

"Haven't you done enough to Colbon already?"

"What do you mean by that?"

"You know what I mean. You broke up his home. You kept . . ."

Walt's face turned dark. His hand slid across the calf of his leg. He resisted the temptation. Instead, he sprang, swinging the heel of his palm to Tom's jaw. Tom saw the blow coming, but he couldn't avoid it. It landed with a *slap* that could be heard inside the bunkhouse. Tom hit the dirt, seat first.

Men came running to see what was wrong. It was for the benefit of these that Walt spoke.

"Tommy, I've always promised I'd make a man out of you, and this is lesson number one. Or haven't you got guts enough to get up from the ground?"

Tom got up. He had always been a trifle scared of Walt but the blow had temporarily knocked the fear out of him. It looked like a fair match. Tom was not so tall or heavy as Walt, but he was quick, and his youth was in his favor. Walt waited for him, the old, contemptuous smile twisting the corners of his mouth.

"Come on, Tommy. I'll spot you the next one. See if you have enough to dump me like you did over at the schoolhouse."

Tom swung a left. He expected one of Walt's fists to fly at the last moment, but Walt kept his hands resting, and only weaved the fraction that was necessary to take the sting from the blow.

Tom came around with a right. Walt moved with it, and drove his left to Tom's midriff. The right followed, a brutal blow that mashed Tom's lips and made his head buzz.

He was on his heels, trying to smash Walt back. He was swinging blindly while Walt was cool and deadly, placing his blows where he wanted them.

A left brought Tom up short. Walt let a haymaker graze his cheek, then he set his heels and delivered one that put Tom in the dirt.

By all the cards in Walt's deck, men who took that punch went down and stayed down. But Tom rolled to hands and knees, spitting dirt and blood, and charged, catching Walt in the middle with his shoulder. He carried Walt to the bunkhouse wall. They slammed and rebounded. The action seemed to clear Tom's head a little. He let go and ripped up a right that turned Walt's eyes to glass and made his knees wobble.

A left followed. Another right. Walt got loose and retreated. His feet tangled with an old horse collar. He fell. He twisted to one side and came up with the heavy collar in his hand. Tom tried to fend off the thing as Walt swung it but it grazed his head and drove with punishing impact against his neck.

He went down on hands and knees. Walt booted him to his back. He was helpless but Walt did not stop. He kicked him alongside the head. A couple of the boys ran over to stop what looked like murder. But Walt had not lost his head. He was perfectly aware of his actions. He kicked Tom once more and turned to face the cow-puncher who was shouting at him.

"What's the matter, Hays?"

"You'll kill that kid."

"I'll make a man of him. And just for sticking your nose into my family affair, you can draw your time."

"My saddle's already in the wagon. I wouldn't work for an outfit where you were boss."

Hays was a top hand. He could nudge a beef herd to the railroad fifty miles away, and do it so easily they would pick up tallow on the way. Walt cooled a trifle.

"Forget it, Hays."

"I heard you the first time. I'll draw my pay."

Walt paid him off. The boys had dragged Tom over to the wash trough and pumped water over his bleeding face. He was still groggy.

"How do you feel?" Walt asked, trying to smile like he'd just been teaching Tom a lesson for his own good.

Tom mumbled something.

"Tom, you're going up north to take over the Flying W."

The Flying W was a big spread that Roose had bought a couple of years ago.

"Why?" Tom asked in a rasping voice between puffed lips.

"It doesn't need to make a damned bit of difference to you. I'm running this outfit and I say you go to the Flying W."

"And I say you can go to hell."

Walt was on the point of starting for him again, then he decided to hear his half-brother out. Through the bunkhouse door Tom could see Hays packing his war sack.

"It doesn't look like I was the only one who couldn't stomach you."

Walt sneered: "I didn't think you'd be able to take your beating like a man."

"Someday," Tom said, "I'll be back for more."

# IV

Tom decided to stay around a while in hopes Roose would get better. Next morning he was about the same. The doc said he might linger like that for months. Tom caught his big Appaloosa horse that Roose had given him on his last birthday, rolled up some belongings in a Cree parfleche, stuck his new carbine in the saddle scabbard, and started out toward the south. He saw Walt down by the bunkhouse watching him. Neither man made a sign of farewell.

The Mexican cattle had moved off the Arrow bench. He saw no sign of them except for the hoof-punched mud around the drying water holes.

The line shack door stood open, and a family of pack rats had moved in. Walt must have sent over for Blamey.

Tom spent the night there. In the morning he baked squaw bread over a sagebrush fire in the little stove. The sun came up, making the room insufferable with heat. He caught his horse, and was just pulling the latigo tight, when the sound of a gunshot came to his ears.

He listened for several minutes. The shooting continued, shots spaced a quarter or half a minute apart. Several miles off. It sounded like somebody target shooting—then a thought came that made his young face turn grim.

He swung up and set out for the Arrow. The shooting kept up. He pulled up at the edge of some bald-faced banks and scanned the flats below. Mexican steers were milling around pretty wildly. Here and there one was down. Two men were shooting, and taking time to make each cartridge count.

Tom followed an old buffalo trail to the bottom. The men were watching him. They were Axel Colbon and a half-breed boy who worked for him. Colbon walked forward a few steps, his Winchester in the crook of his arm, while Tom reined his horse tightly to hold him steady against the smell of fresh blood.

"You're being a damned fool, Axel," he said.

"What do you intend to do about it?"

"Not a thing. I don't ride for the brand any more."

He could tell that Axel didn't believe him.

"Dad had a stroke and he can't last long. Walt has taken over. He called the riders off this herd, that's why they drifted down. I tackled him but he beat hell out of me. I thought I'd better ride down here and tell you he figures on making the squeeze."

"Did you tell him I'd shoot every steer that came down?"

"You'll need lots of cartridges."

"I suppose you think I should take it lying down!"

"No . . . but I think I'd talk it over with the association. Shooting the cattle will give Walt the legal excuse he's looking for."

Axel thought for a while, tall, leather-faced, his eyes deep-set with hatred. He pumped an empty cartridge that still had a wisp of smoke in it, took aim, and shot at another steer. Despite the control he was trying to show, he missed. Tom accepted the shot as his answer and started on across the flat.

"Where are you going?" Axel demanded, raising his voice.

"In to see Loney. Maybe she can talk some sense into your head."

The other fellow was Pete Follet, a half-breed boy of thirteen or fourteen. Pete stood with an old Sharps rifle in his hands, half expecting to be called on to shoot it out with this Steckley, but Tom rode by, scarcely glancing at him. Axel caught his horse, cursing under his breath, and followed toward the ranch house.

It was the same house of cottonwood logs that Axel had brought Tania to seventeen years ago, only now it had a floor in it. There were some pole corrals, crossing and re-crossing Arrow Creek, a one-room bunkhouse where the half-breed boy slept, a stock shed, and a cache house standing on stilts that had been covered with flattened tin cans to resist the claws of marauding skunks.

The two men rode the last couple of miles side-by-side. Loney was in the kitchen, baking bread. If Tom had actually intended to talk to her about Axel's action in shooting the cattle, he forgot about it. They ate dinner.

Afterward Axel said: "Those Mexican steers are still on my grass, Steckley."

"There's only one answer. You small ranchers will have to band together. Lutz, Hoffstabel, Jim Smith, and yourself. Maybe you and Smith will object to those other two because they're nesters with a fancy for sheep, but I wouldn't let that worry me. Build a drift fence and keep it patrolled. If Walt gets to cutting wire, you'll have something to talk about in court."

"It would be next year before we could get enough barbed wire strung to do us any good."

"You can drive 'em back and make out somehow. It'll be better than paying for cattle you've made wolf bait out of."

It was level-headed advice and Axel knew it. He already regretted the shooting business of that morning. He started out with Tom and the half-breed boy to help him, and spent the afternoon running those Mexican steers down the Arrow. By sundown they were scattered from hell to breakfast, and a long way from anything that could be called good grass.

They rode back within sight of the line shack. The almost smokeless haze of a sagebrush fire was coming from the stovepipe.

"Cal Lotts!" said Tom.

He didn't try to hide his feelings about Cal. He spoke the name with a hatred that brought a sharp glance from Axel.

"I hear you had trouble with Cal."

"Someday," said Tom, "I'll kill him."

"Careful, Tom. Killings always come in pairs and have triplets. It's like killing a rattler. There's always another to come and coil up by his dead body."

Tom knew it was Cal Lotts up in that line shack. He always prided himself in being able to build that kind of a fire. Smokeless. There's an art to it—selecting the right sagebrush, getting each twig to blazing before the next is added, keeping the draft so moisture won't form in the middle. It was an art that rustlers and longriders learn. Probably his sidekick, Lester Chadwick, was up there with him. He wondered what they had up their sleeves.

A mellow sunset covered the country and turned the windowpanes of the ranch house to yellow flame as they rode up and unsaddled. Loney set the supper table in the screened-in back porch. There was fresh-baked bread, stewed jerk beef, and canned tomato pooch.

It was getting dark when supper was over. Axel lighted a splinter in the stove and carried it to the kerosene lamp.

"I wouldn't light that if I were you," Tom said.

Axel tossed the splinter back in the stove. "Is Lotts that kind of a gunman?"

"If Walt sent him out to do a job, I guess Cal would do it the easiest way."

For a long time there was a light streak in the western horizon but the valley of Arrow Creek was dense with darkness. Pete Follet, Axel's only cowpuncher, kept nervously creeping outside to peer in the direction of the line shanty.

"What do you think he'll do?" Loney asked, her warm young voice sounding unexpectedly close in the darkened room.

"Cal Lotts? Hard to say. Ride back to the ranch and tell Walt about the cattle, unless he already has his instructions."

"We might as well go to bed," said Axel. But he

did not move. He rolled a cigarette, lifted a lid from the stove to light it from a lingering coal, the reddish glow of it bringing to life the strong lines of his face.

A horse snorted in the piney pasture. Tom stepped out on the front porch. He could see a silvery streak of creek, the dark masses of bunkhouse, horse sheds, and box elder trees. Men were riding up the trail. Three riders, or maybe four.

Axel came and stood at his elbow. "Someone coming?"

"Yes."

"You better stay out of sight. This is my party."

He stamped out his cigarette and went back inside. He was already carrying his Colt, but he armed himself with a Winchester, too. Tom went back to the shadow of the porch and drew his own Winchester from the scabbard. Pete Follet got behind a rain barrel with his Sharps.

"Take it easy, Pete," Tom said. "Don't unwind with that cannon unless I tell you to."

"Yah!" Pete grinned, showing his white teeth.

Loney was at the door. "Don't let Axel go out there alone," she whispered. "They'll kill him."

"He'll take care of himself from the front all right, Loney. It's his back he'll need to worry about with Cal on the job, and I'm here to watch that. You go back inside."

Horses were splashing across the shallow ford.

There was a *jingle* of bit chains, the *click-clack* of a steel shoe on pebbles. A single horseman was coming up the rise of ground from the creek. The others must have stayed back there some place.

His silhouette became visible—a tall man, stooped. A little mannerism he had of swinging his left elbow told Tom it was Cal Lotts. He came with no effort to conceal himself. About a stone's throw from the house he drew up.

"Colbon!" he shouted.

"What do you want?"

Lotts jumped as though the back of his neck had been bullet burned when Colbon's voice sounded so close beside him. He lifted his elbows high to show he was not reaching for his gun. Then he reined around and looked down on Colbon who was walking slowly toward him.

"You don't need that rifle, Colbon. I came here peaceful."

"What do you want?"

"Walt Steckley wants to talk to you."

"Then tell him to come up where I can see him."

"He's at the ranch."

"What does he want to see me about?"

"He wants to talk over this Arrow range with you so there'll be no more trouble."

"There's nothing to talk about. It's mine. I intend to hold it."

"He'll make you an honest offer."

"You can tell Steckley to go to hell."

"Maybe I'll tell him about the way you slaughtered his steers, too."

"Of course, you'll tell him. I want you to tell him as damned quick as you can get there."

"That's the thanks a man gets for tryin' to shoot square with some people." Cal chuckled. "Walt's too easy. Lots of fellows would come out here and burn powder."

"Get moving!"

"Sure," said Cal, making no move to start. "You can wait till I roll a cigarette, can't you?"

He must have been rolling one—it was too dark for Tom to see. He lighted a match. After the long darkness, its flame seemed very bright. Lotts was sitting there, one knee hooked over the saddle horn in a manner that brought his right-hand gun in position where the shortest of motions would have unholstered it. Axel carried his Winchester in the crook of his arm, thumb on the hammer. Someone was moving back there by the creek.

Cal flipped the match away, and Tom half expected him to continue his motion, draw, and make a play for it there. But the layout of the cards didn't quite suit him. He pressed with a bridle rein and the hackamore-trained horse turned dutifully toward the creek.

He jogged out of sight over the bank twenty or thirty yards away. His companions should be down there and it would be natural for him to say something to them, but no word was spoken. A sudden suspicion brought Tom forward. He peered into the dark but the only movement came from Axel Colbon, turning, Winchester still in the crook of his arm.

"Axel!" he shouted.

Whether the warning moved him or whether he had received some hint of treachery, Axel flung himself face foremost to the ground. At the same instant, guns cut loose from three spots, ripping the air above him with murderous cross-fire.

Tom was at the edge of the house, pumping his carbine at the gun flashes. Pete was on his belly, reloading and firing his old, single-shot Sharps.

Tom was a trifle blinded by the flame of his own gun. He was unable to locate Axel. He wondered if a bushwhacker's bullet had cut him down. Then Axel's Winchester cut loose from behind a wagon box.

Cal and his men were falling back, firing each shot from a new position. One of their bullets tore splinters from a porch pillar close to Tom's cheek. There seemed to be an extra gun popping nearby. Loney was shooting through the open door with a .25-20 coyote gun.

Finally the shooting stopped and Tom heard the sound of hoofs hurrying away.

"Anybody get hurt?" Axel asked.

"We're all right."

"I didn't think Walt would get this tough. Not for a while, anyhow."

Tom was doing some thinking. It wasn't exactly Walt's type of move. Walt pulled things that seemed hot-headed but mostly they were planned in advance. He was the kind who liked to bluff—with an ace in the hole. Tom couldn't help but think that his own being here at Colbon's had something to do with it. Perhaps Walt saw him go, guessed his destination, and decided that, if Colbon should turn up killed, it would be blamed on Tom.

Anyhow, Tom kept his opinion to himself. He rolled down his soogins in the bunkhouse beside the half-breed boy.

In the morning Tom talked with Jim Smith.

"We're not in it alone," Jim said. "There are plenty of small ranchers around the Eagle Rocks and north that aren't scared of Walt Steckley. But where the hell do you come in on this, Tommy?"

"Do you suspect me?"

"No, but the others will."

It was the truth, of course. Tom knew better than to ride out to see them. Anyhow, he was no crusader. He was a Steckley. He'd already done a hell of a lot more than most men would. He was tempted to head in for a touch of night life at Fort Benton or Grass Valley, but the face of Loney Colbon drew him back to the Arrow.

He had been at the house scarcely an hour when Sheriff Tad Cameron rode out from Grass Valley.

259

Cameron was a big, bluff man who had been sheriff ever since the county was organized.

"You're in a hell of a mess over those steers!" he bellowed as he dismounted in front of the door. "You ought to have your head examined, Axel. Walt Steckley is in town, mad as a rattlesnake on a hot griddle, swearin' he'll law you for every dollar you got."

"Is that why you're here?"

"Yep, I got to take you in."

"Right now?"

Cameron sniffed. "Well, not till I've tried some of Loney's new bread."

Cameron spent the night there. When he awoke, Axel Colbon had already caught and curried his cayuse driving team, and was backing them against the trees.

"Takin, the gal in with you, Axel?" Cameron asked.

Axel nodded.

"That's a good idea. You'll probably be messin' around with this thing for a couple of weeks. You know how lawsuits are. What lawyer you aim on havin'?"

"I hadn't thought of it."

"Walt's taken on J.B. Rance from Fort Benton. You could get Currell, but he'd likely get you hung. Now, my son-in-law, Lobel Stevens, has set up business at Grass Valley. He's young but he's sure one hell of a talker. . . ."

"I'll take him on."

"That won't be a mistake. You couldn't find twelve jurors in the country but what half of 'em know Lobel and like him. They'd be sure enough anxious to see him win his first case."

It was an all-day trip to Grass Valley—Axel and Loney in the rig, Cameron and Tom riding alongside. They could see the town down in the flats for many hours before reaching it. It was parched, and unpainted, and false-fronted, built chiefly along a single street that was closed at one end by a frame courthouse, and at the other by a large, unpainted livery stable.

Sitting by itself was the depot of the Jim Hill–controlled Montana Central and, beyond that, a vast area of stockyards, now empty awaiting the beef roundup.

Axel jiggled the lines, rousing his tired team to a brisk trot, for it was the custom for a man to put on some little show when arriving, even if he was in the hands of the law. There weren't many on the street, but they all waved to him, strangers and acquaintances alike. Cameron dropped off at the courthouse to round up his son-in-law and Judge Milburn, while Axel put up his team and got rooms at the Territorial Hotel.

# V

Judge Milburn set the bail at $500. The signature of Tom Steckley was accepted without question. The hearing was set for next day and the trial for the following Saturday. Walt Steckley demanded damages totaling $6,000 which was about $4,000 more than Axel Colbon could ever hope to pay. Taking the advice of Lobel Stevens, a vigorous young man who had read law in the offices of Senator Carter down in Helena, Colbon instituted a counter suit for an equal amount, charging range damage by Steckley's cattle.

On Friday the town started filling up. Small ranchers rode in from as far as the Little Sag to the east, and the Marias to the west, for they recognized this as more than just a contest between two men who hated each other on account of a woman. It was a contest between a big rancher and a little rancher. It was a test to see if a big rancher could force the hand of a little one, and then, when he struck back, sue him out of business.

The courtroom filled early Saturday morning. It was suffocating with every seat occupied and men crowded shoulder to shoulder along the walls. Finally, Cameron *clomped* in and boomed out an announcement that the case had been settled by agreement of the rival attorneys. Rumor supplied the details. Walt Steckley, viewing the unexpected wave of sentiment against him, had backed down rather than risk an unfavorable decision. The Steckleys, Walt was quoted as saying, had always been able to take care of their rights without the help of a flock of damned lawyers.

Tom left the judge's office with Axel and Loney. Axel said: "I'm going to hitch up and get back to the ranch. You better come along to the livery stable with me, Tom."

"Sorry, Axel."

Axel didn't argue. He understood. Tom could not sneak out the back way. The town was wondering what would happen when he ran into Walt and it was up to him to give them their satisfaction. That, or be branded a coward.

Loney took hold of his arm. "Tom! Leave your gun here."

"I can't do that."

He left them at the door and started up the plank sidewalk. He met a couple of Milliron cowpunchers who invited him in for a drink. He shook his head.

"Looking for Walt?" one asked.

"Where is he?"

"Up at the Territorial."

"Drinking?"

"He's had a few."

Walt never got really drunk. His wire-tough

body resisted alcohol. It just made him mean.

Tom went on. He knew people were following. He wondered what would happen when they met. Perhaps he could face him out, and that would be the end of it. Perhaps they would fight with their fists. He wasn't afraid of Walt now. Not in a physical way. Not after feeling Walt's knees buckle when his right-hand blow landed that morning at the ranch. The six-shooter at his hip— that was the problem. Maybe he should have left it with Loney. He could never shoot Walt. Not his own half-brother.

Cal Lotts was perched on the cover of a stale-smelling water barrel in front of the Territorial. He watched as Tom approached, smiling through that off-center mouth of his, his buckteeth showing. He snapped shut the buckhorn stockman's knife he was whittling with, letting it fall in his vest pocket. He wore a new pair of checked trousers, and they folded unnaturally where the tie strings of his holsters were cinched around his skinny calves.

This was the first time they had come face to face since that day back at the Arrow line shack. A lot of people had heard about Cal's coming out at the wrong end of the rope and his reputation had suffered accordingly. As a result Tom half expected him to go for his guns. But he didn't.

Cal sneered: "Hello, Tommy. How's the nester's friend?"

"The last time I saw you," said Tom, "you were trying to bushwhack a man. Is that how you decorated those gun butts of yours?"

"You know damned well it wasn't!"

Lotts's right hand kept opening and closing a few inches above that right-hand six-gun. He glanced over his shoulder at the batwing doors leading to the Territorial bar. He was evidently wishing Walt would come out. The babble of voices in there had quieted a little. Tom turned to enter when he heard the sound of heavy boots crossing the floor. The step had a quality he recognized.

Walt came outside, took in the scene with one glance. He'd had a few drinks, there was no mistake about that. The liquor showed in the high color of his face, the extra sharpness of his eyes. He stood with hands rubbing his hips, his wide-slashed mouth twisted down at the corners looking like he had that day back at the Vintner Creek schoolhouse when he was planning to bully Axel Colbon into making a play for his gun. Walt spoke, being sure to make his voice loud enough for people to hear a long way down the street.

"You, Tommy! I thought you'd be too yellow to face me."

"I'm not afraid of you, Walt."

Tom made a motion to unbuckle his gun belt but Walt only twisted his mouth down the farther.

"No, Tommy. I'll not dirty my fists on you

again. I did that once. I tried to make a man of you, but you bit me in the back."

Walt spoke slowly. He spat his words as though they were venom. As he talked, he moved back a trifle, keeping his right thumb hooked in the band of his pants just over the butt of his gun.

Tom could see what he wanted. "I don't want to shoot it out with you, Walt. Neither of us wants to be branded like Cain in the Bible. . . ."

"You talk like a sky pilot."

"Think of old Roose back there. . . ."

"Talk about Roose, you pup! After you've sold your own family out to a bunch of cheap nesters who are figuring on cutting the range with barb wire. . . ."

"Drop your gun, Walt, and I'll drop mine!"

"You take after your mother! She was always a money-grabbin' . . ."

Tom started for him, but Walt backed farther, hand ready, hovering over the butt of his gun.

"Stop it, Walt. By God, I'll . . ."

"You'll what? You'll kill me?"

"We're brothers. We can't settle it with guns."

"You're no brother of mine. Do you hear that? Your mother found you out in the sagebrush. Go for your gun, Tommy!"

Tom moved—stopped. Walt had spun into action. Men were shouting and going for cover. Walt paused, gun two-thirds out of the holster. Tom lifted his hands clear. He looked sick. He couldn't shoot it out with him. Not when he was full of whiskey, anyway.

"Why, you coyote pup!" Walt snarled.

Cal Lotts laughed.

Tom turned abruptly and started back up the sidewalk. Men came from behind fire barrels, and hitching posts, and doorways, crowding in again. Tom stepped over a hitch rack and started cutting across the street. It seemed like his boots were filled with lead. He could hear Walt back there, cursing him. He walked on, hurrying a little. A girl screamed—Loney. He looked up and saw her. She was running toward him from the livery barn.

"Tom! Look out!"

He turned. Walt was aiming down the sights of his gun. Tom started sidewise. Walt fired at Tom's knees. It struck high, tearing through the flesh of his thigh.

The heavy slug knocked his leg from under him. He fell, fingers digging the alkali dust of the street. Walt was cursing, drawing down again. He decided against it, and thrust the pistol in its holster.

The shock had made Tom dizzy for a second. He looked up and there was Loney bending over him.

"I'm sorry," he said. "Maybe I haven't got any guts. I kept thinking of old Roose back there at the ranch . . . I guess I'm just a coward."

"You're not a coward," she kept whispering. "You're not a coward. . . ."

The .45 slug left an ugly tear in the muscles of Tom's leg. He managed to hobble to Axel's rig and pull himself to the box. Doc MacArdle came around and bound it up, but he couldn't talk Tom into staying in town.

During the afternoon, as the rig joggled along the rough prairie road, the leg stiffened up until he had a hard time sitting to drink when Loney held the water jug to his lips. He fell into a feverish sleep, filled with the little, tag ends of nightmares. At last Axel woke him. The stars were dimming with early morning. They were at the ranch house on the Arrow.

He was down with the leg for a week, then the stiffness started to leave, and he was able to get around with a crutch that Axel had sawed out for him.

The hot days of August passed, and a circuit rider working for the roundup association came around to notify Axel of a meeting scheduled for the following week in Grass Valley.

"I suppose they're calling me six varieties of yellow belly in there since my round with Walt," Tom said to Axel when he got back.

"Why, some of 'em do, I suppose. And some of 'em must understand how you felt. There's worse things than being named a coward, I guess. I was called a coward one time and lived through it. And if I had it to do over again, I'd act just the same. There's some problems that you can't settle with a two hundred grain slug of lead."

"My leg's pretty fair now, Axel. I'm going to saddle and ride."

"You're not hangin' around for the roundup then?"

"No."

Axel did not argue with him although it was plain he thought Tom should stay and face it out.

"I'll be back, Loney," Tom said, stopping at the porch before riding away.

Loney looked like she wanted to cry. He could tell she thought he was never coming back.

He rode down the Arrow for a few miles, turned, and took the old Army trail through the wild country of the Missouri River breaks. He crossed the river that was scarcely belly deep at that season of the year, and climbed to the shelf of bench land over south. He spent the night at a little spring near the Shonkin, and shortly after noon next day he rode across the new wagon bridge to Fort Benton.

In a country of new towns with their mushroom architecture, Fort Benton seemed stable and old. There were the large warehouses of the I.G. Baker and Coulson steamboat lines by the river, and beyond them a business district of wood, brick, and cut stone dominated by the Grand Union Hotel whose sign, in genuine gold leaf, offered the choice of American or European plans. On higher ground, set against a background of barren clay hills, were the turreted mansions of families whose names were already old in this raw, new land.

The Grand Union was definitely not the type of place into which one rode his horse, which was more than could be said for the Territorial up at Grass Valley. Tom dismounted, and a Negro boy ran out.

"Unsaddle yo' horse, Mist' Steckley?" he asked.

Ordinarily it would have pleased Tom to be remembered, but not today. He wished no one would recognize him. He went inside the cool lobby. Its plush, and leather, and potted palms made him feel dusty and out of place.

"Your old corner room, Mister Steckley?" asked the shiny-headed clerk, dipping a pen.

Tom signed and went upstairs, letting a second Negro boy tote his parfleche. He washed and went back down for a bottle of St. Louis beer. Cultus George, a big, flashy gambler was there, shaking dice. He looked at Tom with a surprised lift of his eyebrows and came over.

"What are all these lies they've been telling about Walt putting the run on you?"

"Why, it's true," said Tom coldly, leaving his shoulder pointed toward Cultus George, and looking at his beer bottle.

"I know how it was, kid. You just didn't want to

load your own brother up with lead. That's what I told the boys when they was namin' you forty kinds of coyote. I said . . ."

"Let's not talk about it."

"Sorry." Cultus George moved back to the end of the bar.

Tom finished his beer. It was a temptation just to go up to his room. Crawl in his hole. Instead, he made the rounds. Facing people made him feel better.

In the morning he saddled and headed for the Highwoods. By evening he was at the Tompkins Ranch where the western end of the Missouri River roundup was being outfitted.

This Missouri River roundup was a big one, covering the vast country almost to the mouth of the Milk, 100 miles from the Dakota line. Riders were there from as far south as Wyoming, looking for a winter grubstake from the wages these big outfits paid to get in the beef. Their talk smacked of the trail—of a raid on Jackson's Hole, of the shooting of Curly Stevens down in Mandan, of the activities of the redcoats near Whoop-Up. It was a relief to find the Steckleys of scant importance.

# VI

Tom was with the bunch working the wide sagebrush flats east of the Judith when he heard the news about Axel Colbon. Rusty Meigs, a range tramp and saddle blanket gambler, had ridden over from the Cow Island crossing. He was squatted by the cook fire, a tin cup of scalding coffee in his hand, talking. He stopped talking abruptly when Tom walked up.

"Hello Rusty," Tom said, ladling stew into a tin plate.

Rusty returned the greeting while blowing at his coffee. There were ten or twelve other boys hunkered there, all of them quiet.

"Ain't you heard the news, Tom?"

"What news?"

"About your brother and Colbon."

"No."

"They had a gunfight. Axel's dead."

Tom went back to the gravy end of the chuck wagon and put down his plate. The news had been so sudden it froze him inside. He thought about Loney, wondering where she was, how she was taking it. And he cursed himself. He should have shot it out with Walt. He should have killed him.

"When was it?" he asked, making his voice sound calm.

"Late yesterday, I guess. I wasn't up there. I was

on the Cow Island trail headed over here when one of the Milliron boys told me about it. It seems like the roundup wagon was camped at Corwin Springs. The two of 'em, Axel and Walt, had been gettin' on about the same as usual . . . that is to say, they was givin' each other the wide leave alone. Supper was over, and Walt started over to the buckboard, when he run into Axel. The two of 'em must have had words, and that's when the shootin' commenced. I guess Axel went for his gun first. That's what the witnesses said, anyhow."

"Who were the witnesses?"

"Well, there was just one, as far as anybody can find out. It was Cal Lotts."

Rusty spoke the name significantly, probably aware of the effect it would have on Tom Steckley.

"You didn't hear anything about the girl . . . Loney?"

"Why, no. All I heard was just what I told you."

Tom poured a cup of coffee. He drank slowly, trying not to show the emotions that were shaking him.

"I'll have to be leaving you," Tom said to Preddy, the sub-captain for that end of the roundup.

Preddy nodded. "I'll have Vandergoot make out your check and mail it to you."

An early morning mist was rising from the Missouri when he reached it near the mouth of the Judith. He forded the river and headed across plains where sagebrush grew belly high. The country rose a little, and with dawn he could make out the purplish gash of Rock Creek, winding down from the Eagle Rocks country, and farther away the smaller marks of Vintner Creek, Elk Creek, and Corwin Springs.

The country seemed to be worked clean of cattle, and he got to wondering if the roundup camp had moved on. In the late afternoon he sighted two riders working the tableland north of the breaks. A dust veil suspended in the clear atmosphere turned pinkish as the sun sank low. He knew then that the camp had not moved.

A six-shooter barked from the direction of some blackish rocks to the south. He pulled in and waited as a rider came toward him. He recognized Cass Rutledge, one of the Steckley cowpunchers.

"I had a hunch it was you," said Cass. "You headin' up there?"

Tom nodded.

"Loney is goin' up Vintner Crick in a rig. Thought you might like to know."

"You talk to her?"

"It wasn't me that seen her. Wilson sighted her through the glasses."

"Where's her father?"

"We buried him."

"What was the straight of it, Cass?"

"Why, I don't know that. Cal was supposed to be the only one that saw it."

"What do you mean . . . *supposed?*"

"Blamey and White drew their time and lit out the same night. They were both in camp when it happened. Something funny about it. But don't tell Walt I told you so."

"I won't get you in trouble."

Tom headed southwest in hopes of intercepting Loney. He came to the trail leading up from Vintner Creek. It was hoof trodden by cattle, but cutting through the roughened dirt were the unbroken impressions of a wagon track. He followed it straight into the roundup camp.

No one paid much attention as he rode in through herds of bawling, dust-kicking cattle. There was a big fire between the two chuck wagons. He caught sight of Loney's rig.

"Walt!" somebody shouted.

Clifton, one of the Steckley cowpunchers, was coming toward him. Clifton stopped suddenly. "Oh, it's you, Tom!"

The mistake jolted Tom a little, although this was not the first time he'd been taken for Walt. Clifton watched as Tom touched the Appaloosa with his spurs and rode on.

After talking with Cass Rutledge, Tom had prayed to see Loney so he could head her off from the camp. But now that she was there, he just as desperately wanted to avoid her. Until after he had settled this thing with Walt, anyhow.

He headed for the chuck wagons. The boys were gathering around, waiting for Buzz Nolan, the cook, to hammer on his iron skillet and shout: "Come on, you mavericks, grub pile!"

He recognized most of them, although a few new hands had drifted in for roundup pay. No sign of Walt, but there was his rig, and his favorite horse was tied to a rear wheel. He couldn't be far. Tom swung down.

For a while he thought he would get by without seeing Loney, but he had not taken four steps when he heard her, shouting his name. He walked on, pretending not to hear, but she shouted again.

She must have been crying all night and most of the day by the look of her eyes. If he needed anything to harden his determination about settling things with Walt, those eyes of Loney's did it.

"Tom, you heard about . . . ?"

"Don't hurt yourself any more, Loney," he said, touching her gently on the arm. "Don't talk about it."

"They buried him already."

"I know. Cass told me. You run along, Loney. You go on back to your rig."

"Tom, you're not planning . . . ?"

"I have to, Loney. I got to, or else stop pretendin' to be a man."

"They'll kill you." She spoke slowly, and her

girlish voice gave her words shocking conviction. "They'll kill you, just like they did Axel. They'll bushwhack you."

"It was a gunfight, wasn't it?"

"That's what they want people to believe, but one of the boys claims that Walt didn't shoot him at all. Cal Lotts was hid back in the shadow waiting for Walt to give the high sign. Blamey and White saw it, and that's why Walt paid them off and got them started out of the country. One of the boys told me that. It was . . ."

"Never mind who it was. You'll get him shot, too. You go back to your rig, Loney."

She stood there and watched him go. It was growing dark, and the flames of the cook fire brought to life the drawn lines of Tom Steckley's face as he walked toward it. He seemed long-jawed tonight, and heavier-legged. The last months had brought maturity to him, and maturity made him look surprisingly like his half-brother Walt. Maybe that was one of the reasons they all stared at him.

"Hello, boys," he said as though he had just ridden in from gathering beef. A mumble ran around the circle of cowboys waiting grub. There wasn't a man there but seemed more nervous than he did.

"Where's Walt?" he asked.

Everyone seemed to be waiting for another to answer. Old Buzz Nolan, the camp cook, broke the uncomfortable moment of silence. "Hello, Lotts!" he called out, looking directly over Tom's shoulder.

His words were intended for a warning. Tom spun around. Lotts was walking up quietly from around the wagon. He stopped, his hands a trifle lower than a peaceful man's hands should be. His eyes were sullen.

"You wouldn't shoot a man in the back, would you, Cal?" Tom asked.

"What do you mean by that?" Cal came up a step or two, looking from Tom to the cowpunchers around the fire, and then back again. He waited for Tom to answer, and, when the answer didn't come right away, he cried, raising his voice testily: "Maybe you're tryin' to say I bushwhacked Axel Colbon!"

"Nobody mentioned Colbon. You must have a bad conscience."

"My conscience will do."

"That's how you engraved your gun handles, isn't it, Cal . . . by shooting men on the sly?"

Lotts tried to laugh, but all he could do was twist that loose mouth of his and show his buckteeth. He caught the expressions around the fire. Everyone knew that Tom had thrown fighting words at him. They expected him to draw. But he couldn't move. Ever since that fracas at the line shanty he had feared Tom Steckley. The fear had lain deeply inside him; he hadn't even admitted it to himself. But it came out in every clammy pore of his body now. He knew he was speedier on the draw, perhaps the better shot. But there is more to fighting than that. There is a thing called nerve that weights the odds when the chips are down. And tonight, when Cal Lotts should have been calm and deadly, he was only turned sick with a fear of death.

"I don't want to hurt you, Tommy," he said with a painful attempt at swagger. "I don't want to beat Walt out of the chance."

"It's like I said that day back in the bunkhouse . . . you talk kill all the time but you haven't the guts to shoot it out face to face."

Cal started as though to get a tin coffee cup from the stack. Tom stepped in front of him. Cal tried to move out of the way. He took a step back. He looked sick, like a man suffering from ptomaine. Tom slapped him. The blow snapped his head to one side. He went down, throwing his hands back into the dirt to catch himself.

One of his guns fell to the ground. He made no move to pick it up. He crawled backward on his haunches. Tom picked up the gun and flung it at his face. It struck heavily against the forearm that Cal raised.

"Don't!" he pleaded in a voice that was all buck-teeth and hoarseness. "Don't kill me. I never done anything to you, Tom. I'll get out of the country. I'll catch my horse, and you'll never see me. . . ."

"You killed Colbon."

"No, I didn't. May God strike me dead if I ever . . ."

"You killed him. You bushwhacked him from the shadow while Walt was talking to him."

"Don't. Don't kill me. Listen, Tom. I'll tell you the truth. I never wanted any part of this business. That damned murdering half-brother of yours . . ."

Cal Lotts stopped, and was staring at something beyond the chuck wagon. He gasped a word and started to get to his feet. He wanted to run but his legs weren't functioning. A gunshot split the evening air. There was a *thump* as the heavy bullet connected with Lotts's body. It spilled him back, but he was still alive. He clawed for his remaining gun. Then, wounded and cornered, the slavishness of his fear dropped away. The gun flew to his hand, but a second bullet found its mark and left only a single shudder of life in him.

Tom whirled around. There was Walt with a gun in his hand. By the light of the cook fire, Tom could see a wisp of powder smoke trailing up from the muzzle. Walt's lips twisted down at the corners in his old, contemptuous smile.

"It was me who shot Axel Colbon! I shot it out with him. I gave him what he's been asking for!"

"You're a liar, Walt. You talked to him while this hired snake of yours shot him from ambush, and every man in this camp knows you did."

Steckley could see that suspicion on every face. It enraged him. He cursed, and swung the muzzle of his .45. It roared, sending a spit of burning powder. Tom plunged, headfirst, across the ground.

The extending tongue of the chuck wagon was a moment's protection. Walt shifted. It gave Tom the fraction of a second he needed. He rolled over, fired with one elbow propped on the ground.

The bullet struck low, turning Walt half around, smashing him back. He was down on hands and knees with the cook's plunder box in the way. Tom sprang up in time to see Walt stagger to the partial protection of the wagon wheels.

There was a wild stampede of men to clear the line of fire. The air rocked with five shots spaced so closely that two seconds would have covered them. When they were finished, Tom was still on his feet. Walt was down behind the wheel. He was rolling his head, trying to rise. There was a bullet wound in his hip, another near his heart.

"Better get him inside the wagon," Tom said to old Wes Geary. "Pull his boots off. I think he'd rather have it that way."

Nobody thought Walt would last out the hour, but at the end of that time he was stronger than ever.

"I'll come around and shoot his lights out yet," he told Wes Geary who was in the wagon with him. "They can't prove anything on me no matter what that yellow Cal Lotts tried to say. I shot it out with Colbon toe to toe."

"Sure," said Wes in a tone that called Walt a liar.

In the morning, Sheriff Tad Cameron rode into camp.

"Where's Walt Steckley and Cal Lotts?"

Buzz Nolan answered: "Why, we buried poor Cal last night, but Walt's yonder in the wagon."

"Tell him to come out."

"Walt ain't in much shape to travel."

Tom came up. "What do you want of him?"

"I'm here to arrest him for murder."

"Whose murder?"

"Axel Colbon."

"How did you know?"

"Why, I keep my ears open. Blamey and White blew into town yesterday with more money than they ever had in their lives. First off, they said they were headed for Canada, and then they decided to stick around long enough to paint the town. Well, you know how whiskey works on a weak mind, and before sundown they spilled the works. It seems like they came up just as Walt and Cal bushwhacked Axel. It was Walt that pulled the trigger. Walt saw 'em, and gave 'em each a year's pay to get out of the country. I got 'em locked in the stone shack to make sure they'll be around when it comes time to testify. You can't hang a man without eye witnesses . . . that's what my son-in-law, Lobel Stevens, says."

Brother John, a traveling sky pilot, said a few words over the grave of Axel Colbon that day, and the boys stood around with their hats off, feeling mighty sorry for Loney.

"But it ain't like she had nobody to take care of her," said Charley Jesrud, the Steckley outrider. "Tom will take over that job without an argument, and, unless I miss my cards, old Roose will be mighty glad to have her for a daughter-in-law now that he's got over his stroke enough to sit up and cuss the grub."

Tom Steckley hitched the rig, and climbed to the seat beside Loney. They drove through herds of bawling cattle, across a mile of level prairie, and down the incline toward Vintner Creek where they were beyond sight of the roundup camp.

Tom took Loney's small hand in his. "Loney, I never could ask you before because I was scared it could never be. But Loney, you know how I feel about you. And will you . . . ?"

"Yes, Tom," she whispered. "The answer is yes."

Like iron drawn to a magnet, her strong, young form came to him, and her lips, like her answer, were eager and waiting.

# About the Author

**Dan Cushman** was born in Osceola, Michigan, and grew up on the Cree Indian Reservation in Montana. He graduated from the University of Montana with a Bachelor of Science degree in 1934 and pursued a career in mining as a prospector, assayer, and geologist before turning to journalism. In the early 1940s his novelette-length stories began appearing regularly in such Fiction House magazines as *North-West Romances* and *Frontier Stories*. Later in the decade his North-Western and Western stories as well as fiction set in the Far East and Africa began appearing in *Action Stories*, *Adventure*, and *Short Stories*. *Stay Away, Joe*, which first appeared in 1953, is an amusing novel about the mixture, and occasional collision, of Indian culture and Anglo-American culture among the Métis (French Indians) living on a reservation in Montana. The novel became a bestseller and remains a classic to this day, greatly loved especially by Indian peoples for its truthfulness and humor. Yet, while humor became Cushman's hallmark in such later novels as *The Old Copper Collar* (1957) and *Good Bye, Old Dry* (1959), he also produced significant historical fiction in *The Silver Mountain* (1957), concerned with the mining and politics of silver in Montana in the 1890s. This novel won a Spur Award from the Western Writers of America. His fiction remains notable for its breadth, ranging all the way from a story of the cattle frontier in *Tall Wyoming* (1957) to a poignant and memorable portrait of small-town life in Michigan just before the Great War in *The Grand and the Glorious* (1963).

# Additional Copyright Information

**Center Point Large Print**
600 Brooks Road / PO Box 1
Thorndike, ME 04986-0001 USA

**(207) 568-3717**

**US & Canada:**
**1 800 929-9108**
www.centerpointlargeprint.com